SEAL
THE DEAL

JACK SILKSTONE

BOOKS

This book is dedicated to the Military Working Dogs who have served, loyal and steadfast, alongside their handlers in the world's deadliest conflict zones.

Vinci Books

vinci-books.com

Published by Vinci Books Ltd in 2025

1

A CIP catalogue record for this book is available from the British Library.
Paperback ISBN: 9781036703868

The EU GPSR authorised representative is Logos Europe, 9 rue Nicolas Poussion, 17000 La Rochelle, France
contact@logoseurope.eu

By Jack Silkstone

SEAL

SEAL of Approval

SEAL the Deal

Signed SEAL'd and Delivered

Chapter One

Jennifer Reynolds leaned against the hood of her Ford pickup and sipped from a banana, acai and mango smoothie. Tall with a slim athletic build she cut an attractive figure in the khaki and green uniform of an Oregon Parks and Recreation Department Ranger. Her pale blue eyes watched the road out of town from beneath a felt campaign hat. Not one for sunglasses she tended to squint. Which, combined with her upturned nose, full mouth and high cheekbones, gave her a country girl next door look.

A passing pickup tooted its horn and Jenny, as her friends called her, raised her hand and waved. Oakridge, Oregon born and bred she'd left the small town after high school to pursue a career in law. Ten years later she was back having abandoned a corporate salary to pursue her childhood dream job.

As she finished the smoothie an SUV pulled out of the parking lot behind her and stopped alongside. The window lowered revealing a blonde woman in her late fifties.

"Hi Darlene," said Jenny.

"Afternoon, darlin'," replied the woman in a southern drawl. "Is class still on at five?"

Jenny nodded. "Yeah, but next month it changes to six. Sam is switching up the rosters."

Darlene smiled. "Don't you go canceling on us. Those classes are just the dandiest. I've got two new girls comin' along tonight."

"The more, the merrier."

"I haven't felt this fit since I was running track at Oklahoma State." She leaned out of the window and whispered. "And, ever since I got that home pole, Steve and I have been at it like jackrabbits."

Jenny laughed.

"No, seriously. It's done wonders for my confidence. I never thought pole dancing could be so therapeutic."

"I'm glad to hear that."

The radio on Jenny's equipment belt crackled. "Reynolds, you there?"

She recognized her boss Sam's voice. "Darlene, I have to take this."

The woman waved. "I'll see you tonight."

Jenny watched her drive away as she lifted the radio to her mouth. "Sam, Reynolds here."

"Jenny, can you shoot over to the Country Club. They've got a bear stuck in one of their dumpsters."

"Again? Seriously boss, do they ever fasten them?"

"Clearly not. Brian says it's only a little fellow. You'll be able to handle it, right?"

"I'll get over there right now." Jenny stowed the radio and climbed inside the pickup.

She grinned as she drove through the sleepy town and out onto the 58 toward McCredie Springs. A year ago she'd been part of a takeover of a multi-million dollar company.

Now, she was speeding through the rolling tree-covered hills of Lane County to rescue an overly inquisitive black bear. She'd always dreamed of being a park ranger, but she'd been swept up in the pressure to attend college and join the corporate world. Long hours, dealing with endless greed and a failed relationship had been the catalyst to move home and pursue that dream.

The McCredie Springs Country Club was located on the outskirts of the Willamette National Forest, the one and a half million-acre park that Jenny helped manage. Technically it was outside of her jurisdiction, but when it came to wildlife that didn't perturb rangers.

She left the highway and drove along a pine-lined lane and into the opulent grounds. White colonial style villas dotted a landscape of vines, woods, golf greens and fairways. The heart of the estate was a southern mansion that housed the restaurant, day spa and offices. Turning off the main road she passed the swimming pool and stables, heading toward the equipment sheds.

A hundred yards out she spotted one of the bright green police cruisers of the Sheriff's Department. Two uniformed officers were talking to Brian Douglass, the property manager. She parked a distance away and walked across to join them.

She recognized the officers; Ed and Harold had attended the same high school as her, albeit a few years later.

"Well if it ain't Jenny the bear wrestling lawyer from New York." Ed was the mouthier of the two. His hulking partner Harold didn't say much.

Jenny ignored the jibe and approached the manager. "Hi, Brian."

He gave a warm smile. "I'm sorry, Jenny. One of the

staff forgot to fasten the latch. Came out here this morning and found the little fella inside." He gestured to a large dumpster positioned under a tree. "These boys were passing by, but they haven't been much help."

Ed spat in the dust. "Come on, that ain't right. I offered to shoot the damn thing."

Jenny glared at him as she walked across to the dumpster. Lifting the lid she peered inside. A snarl startled her and she dropped it with a clang. Instinctively her hand moved to the butt of the pistol she wore on her belt.

Ed laughed. "What's wrong Jenny? You scared of the little bear?"

Harold laughed.

Jenny exhaled and lifted the lid again.

In the bottom of the steel dumpster sat a young black bear. She guessed its weight at a little over eighty pounds, most likely a female. The shredded remains of trash bags surrounded the animal. It had evidently climbed in looking for food and couldn't grip the smooth sides to get out.

She flipped over the lid triggering aggressive roars from the bear. "Brian, I think it might be the same one as last time."

"Yeah, I figured as much. Once they work out where the food is they keep coming back."

Jenny strode to the bed of her truck where there was a large metal cage. She dropped the tailgate and hefted the cage to the ground. Then she grabbed a pole with a cord on the end of it and a long piece of two by four. "I'm going to relocate her to the park."

Brian took the timber from her. "Good idea. I'd hate to have to destroy her."

Ed watched from a distance. "Be easier to shoot it.

There are plenty of bears in the park and this is a nuisance animal."

Jenny fixed him with an icy look.

"Hey, if I want to shoot it I can. This is Lane County jurisdiction, not National Forest."

She gestured for Brian to join her at the bin. "Shoot it, Ed. See what happens if you do."

"Don't threaten me, Missy," growled the deputy.

She turned to him and smiled. "That's not a threat, it's a promise. You try and destroy that animal and I'll push this pole sideways up your ass." A jiggle of the noose emphasized the point.

Ed scowled and Harold chuckled.

"Shut up idiot," he snapped.

Jenny turned her attention to the bear. "Brian, drop that log in so she can climb it."

The rancher followed her instructions and a moment later the head of the bear appeared over the lip. Jenny hooked the noose over its head and pulled the animal to the ground. Then with Brian's help, she maneuvered it into the transportation cage.

Ed watched from a safe distance, hand resting on the butt of his pistol.

"Don't just stand there. Help us lift the damn crate onto the truck," bellowed Brian.

The deputies helped out but didn't hang around for long. With the bear secure they continued their patrol, leaving Brian and Jenny sharing a Bud Light.

"Useless as all hell. Don't know why the administration staff called them," said the former rancher.

Jenny finished her beer and tossed it in the dumpster. "Well, this little lady shouldn't give you any more trouble." She checked her watch. "I've got enough time to get her back to the station, tagged and out into the park." She climbed into her truck.

"Till next time," Brian shot through her open window.

"Keep those bins closed."

"Yes, ma'am."

Jenny unwrapped her legs from the floor to ceiling pole and lowered herself slowly to the ground. "OK ladies, last move," she shouted over the pumping music.

Around her a dozen women dressed like her, in crop tops and leggings, attempted to replicate the move to varying levels of success. When they had all touched down she killed the music.

"Well done, a great effort by everyone. Let's run through some stretches and wrap it up."

She'd been instructing the small class at a dance studio in Jacksonville for the past six months. In that time it had grown from a few friends to classes of up to twenty women. Word had spread fast. If it continued she was going to need a bigger premises.

Once the warm down was complete Jenny pulled on a pair of track pants and a hoodie.

"Another fantastic session," gushed Darlene as she made to leave.

"You've really progressed," she replied, tying her laces.

"Like I said, getting a pole at home was a smart move."

"Jenny, when are you getting more portable poles?" asked another of the women.

"Yeah, I want one too," added another.

Grinning she grabbed her gear bag. "They should arrive

later in the week. I'll update my Facebook page as soon as they're in."

She left the dance studio and crossed the parking lot to where she'd left her car. On her way she spotted a massive truck parked alongside her Chrysler. A tall figure leaned against the door of a shiny new Ford F-150 Raptor.

She recognized Lieutenant Carter Brown by his trademark Stetson hat and square stubble covered jaw. Dressed in jeans, boots and a check shirt he wore a pistol on his belt. He was the senior officer at the Oakridge Sheriff's station and a former classmate of Jenny's.

He tipped his hat as she approached. "Miss Reynolds, how are you this evening?"

She managed a tight-lipped smile as she took out her keys. "I'm good thanks, Carter."

He stepped away from his truck. "Jenny, look, I dropped by because I wanted to apologize for the way my men acted today. Old man Douglass rang my office and gave me a heads up."

Jenny turned to the handsome police officer and shrugged. "It was nothing. Boys will be boys."

He laughed. "True, but I would like to make it up to you by taking you out to dinner."

"That's a lovely gesture, Carter, but totally unnecessary. I appreciate the courtesy of a face-to-face apology. Thank you, from one professional to another."

He took a step closer and placed his hand on the car door. "Look, all I'm asking for is dinner. We'll grab a steak, my treat. It'll be good for intra-agency relations."

Jenny put her key in the lock. "In that case, you should drop by the ranger station and catch up with Sam and the rest of the crew. Bring Ed and Harold, we'll put on coffee and donuts."

A scowl split his granite features. "I'm not someone you want to make an enemy of."

"No one's trying to make an enemy of you, Carter. I'm just declining your invitation to dinner. As far as I'm aware, that's not a declaration of hostile intent."

"You threatened one of my officers today. I could bring you in for that."

She turned to face him with hands on her hips. "Really? You're going to arrest me based on a flippant comment that was made in jest." She held her wrists out. "Take me in, big shot. I'll take great pleasure in destroying your fantasy in court."

"Just watch yourself, Jenny."

She smiled. "I will."

He turned, opened the door of his pickup and climbed in. The rig rumbled to life and he backed clear before roaring off down the road.

Jenny frowned as she watched the Ford disappear. The Raptor was an expensive truck. Not something a police wage would easily buy. Pushing the thought from her head she climbed into her sedan. She needed to get home, feed her cat, put dinner on and get to bed. The team had an early start in the morning.

A dozen miles out of Oakridge a battered pickup with a bloodhound in the bed was parked beneath a tree on a dirt track. Two men sat inside. Hank, the older of the two, wore jeans, a denim shirt, battered cowboy boots and a ten gallon hat. Carl wore woodland camouflage pants and a stained USMC T-shirt.

Hank held a cell phone to his ear. "Yeah, no worries

we'll get it done." He ended the call and slid the phone into his shirt pocket. Pulling a revolver from his belt he popped the chamber and checked it was loaded.

"So, what's the deal?" asked Carl.

"Travis reckons he's been stealing dope and selling it on the side."

"Shit, that's low. Real low." Carl took out his Glock pistol, cracked the slide and eyeballed the brass cartridge in the chamber. "He want him dead or fucked up?"

"Smith's got kids. So, just a few broken bones to get the point across."

Carl smirked, holstering his pistol as he pulled an extendable baton from the pocket of his combat pants. "Been waiting to try this sucker out."

Hank frowned as he started the truck. "Where the hell did you get that?"

"I bought it online. Got me a sweet deal on a whole bunch of stuff."

"More useless military junk." He dropped the pickup into gear, turned on the headlights and planted his foot on the accelerator.

The truck bounced along the rutted track its lights illuminating thick woods on either side. After half a mile they passed a fence, turned right and stopped in front of a rundown farmhouse.

"I'll handle this. You back me up," said Hank as he killed the engine and donned a pair of thick leather gloves.

"Why am I always the backup?" whined Carl.

He turned with a frown. "Because you're a goddamn fuck up." Climbing from the truck he strode toward the house. As he approached the door opened and a figure clutching a shotgun appeared in the porch light, Andrew Smith.

"Who's out there?"

"Hey, it's Hank and Carl," Hank said as he climbed the steps to the porch, fists clenched by his side.

Smith relaxed and lowered the shotgun. "Oh, hi guys. Thought you might be rustlers. Someone tried to steal some gear outta my barn the other night."

Hank nodded. "Seems to be a lot of that going around." He swung a savage right hook as he reached out and ripped the shotgun from Smith's hands. His fist caught the man on the jaw and he went down like a sack of potatoes.

"Nice punch," said Carl as he joined him.

"Help get him around behind the barn." He lifted the unconscious man by one arm.

Carl took the other and they dragged him past the truck out of the light cast by the porch and behind a dilapidated barn.

They sat him against a wall and Hank slapped him. "Wake the fuck up."

It took a moment for the man to come to. When he did, he tried to climb to his feet. Hank jammed the revolver under his chin. "Sit tight, boy."

"What's this all about?" the man stammered.

"Why don't you tell me?"

Smith stared across at Carl with pleading eyes. "Look, I haven't done anything wrong, I promise."

"That's not what Travis is saying."

The fear dropped from his face, replaced with a look of contempt. "That fat fuck's a liar. What the hell has he told you?"

"Said you've been stealing dope," added Carl.

Hank turned and silenced his partner with a glare. Then he turned his attention back to Smith. "Leg or arm?"

"What?"

He clenched his jaw and hissed through his teeth. "Leg or fucking arm."

Smith stared him in the eye. "You'd take Travis's word over mine?"

"Carl, do both." Hank stepped back, his pistol still aimed at Smith's face.

"Really? You mean it?"

"Just do it."

His partner flicked the extendable baton from his pocket and stepped in over the top of Smith.

"Carl, we've been friends for a long time—"

The sickening crack of his leg snapping cut him off. A blood-curdling scream filled the air as Carl lifted the baton and smashed it into his arm, crushing more bone.

Hank pushed his partner out of the way. "Shut the fuck up. Shut up or I'll shoot you in the goddamn head."

Smith managed to clench his jaw and stifle his cries.

"You see that, Hank? You see that? Barely had to swing the bastard. Did all the work for me."

He turned to his partner. "Shut the hell up and get the truck." Waiting till his partner disappeared he leaned in close. "You tell anyone who did this and you're dead."

The man nodded with his jaw clenched.

"Andy, where are you?" a female voice called from the farmhouse.

"You've paid for your transgression. Things are square. Don't do anything you or your family is gonna regret."

He shook his head. "It wasn't me, Hank."

Hank left him whimpering against the barn strode across to the truck and climbed inside.

"That was fun," said Carl as they drove back down the track.

"You're a sick fuck," he murmured as he took a pinch of chewing tobacco from a tin and stuffed it into his lip.

"Goddamn thief deserved what he got."

"So we're told."

Carl turned to him with a confused look on his face. "If he hasn't been stealing the dope, who has?"

Hank spat into an empty coke bottle. "How the fuck would I know?"

Chapter Two

The beat of rotor blades penetrated the Plexiglas windows of the cockpit and reverberated through Mike Saunders' chest. The square-jawed twenty-nine-year-old wiped his hands on his knees. His palms were sweaty despite the frigid air inside the helicopter. He glanced out the window at the snowcapped mountains and exhaled slowly.

A Navy Special Warfare Operator, the grey-eyed SEAL was a veteran of two major campaigns and a dozen covert operations. He'd spent hundreds of hours in helicopters flying over mountains, jungles, deserts and the ocean. However, never in his career was he ever this nervous. The plan was elaborate. There were so many things that could go wrong.

"How you doing bud?" asked the pilot over his headset.

He raised an eyebrow at the man and gestured over his shoulder at the other passenger.

"You're all good. She can't hear us."

"What's our ETA?" asked Mike.

"Couple more minutes. The guys on the ground have

everything ready. They're standing by for your arrival." He made an adjustment to the aircraft's controls. "So relax and stop looking so damn nervous." He nodded ahead. "OK, we're coming up on our landing zone."

Mike looked through the windshield at the approaching landscape. A boulder-speckled glacier between two high peaks rapidly approached.

He glanced over his shoulder at the passenger in the rear. Ali's green eyes sparkled from inside the hood of a North Face jacket. She wore a broad smile on her elfin features.

"Wow," she mouthed.

Her expression went a long way to easing his nerves. He and Ali had been dating for over a year now. In fact, for the last two months they'd been living together. Mike had never felt this way about anyone. He was totally and utterly in love with the beautiful veterinarian. She was intelligent and kind, but also independent enough to deal with his military career. What's more she adored his dog, Axe. This holiday to the South Island of New Zealand was his way of thanking her for everything she had done for them both.

Smiling he turned his attention back to the terrain ahead. The glacier loomed and a moment later the pilot touched the skids down on the hard packed snow, killing the turbine. "OK kids, this is it. Welcome to the Franz Josef glacier."

Mike stepped from the cabin, opened the rear door for Ali and surveyed the surroundings. Snow-capped mountains stretched out in every direction. In the distance, he could see the coastline and bright blue Tasman Sea.

"It's stunning, babe," she murmured.

Feeling her arms around his waist he turned, wrapped

her in a hug and kissed her. The view lost its magnetism as their lips touched.

A moment later they parted and Mike turned to see the pilot at the nose of the helicopter pretending to inspect the windshield. He looked up, saw they were done and smiled. "OK, lovebirds. If you come with me, I'll show you the best view this side of the equator."

As they followed him across the glacier toward a rocky outcrop Mike's keen eye spotted fresh tracks in the snow. He glanced sideways at Ali; her attention was fixed on the horizon. She turned to him, grinning like a child at Christmas. Then she frowned and cocked her head. "Mike, can you hear that?"

He took her hand. "No, what can you hear?"

Her eyes sparkled. "Music."

Mike's pulse quickened as they rounded the outcrop and the notes of a violin reached his ears.

"You're kidding me." Ali stopped dead in her tracks and squeezed his hand.

A pair of deck chairs sat in the snow. Between them was perched a silver champagne bucket beside a platter of fruit, cheese and caviar. A few yards away a violinist dressed in a tuxedo was playing.

The pilot gestured to the chairs. "Please, take a seat."

Ali sat and the pilot turned waiter, placing a blanket over her legs. Then he poured them each a glass of champagne before disappearing behind the outcrop.

Mike turned to Ali and raised his glass. "To the most incredible person I know."

A tear formed in her eye as she lifted hers. "You're so sweet." She gestured to the view. "This is unbelievable."

His heart raced as he glanced at the violinist. The man nodded and changed the song.

It took a moment for Ali to recognize the tune. "That's 'My Heart Will Go On'." She turned to the musician.

Mike felt like a squadron of butterflies would burst from his stomach as he reached into his pocket. He slipped out of his chair, took her hand and knelt.

Her eyes went wide as he raised the velvet case and snapped it open. "Alison Charlotte Taylor," he said with a waver. "Will you make me the happiest man alive and marry me?"

Tears filled her eyes and she nodded. "Yes, yes. Of course, I will."

As he slipped the diamond ring onto her finger, she leaned forward and kissed him. Their lips touched and Mike felt all the anxiety of the last twenty-four hours replaced by elation. He was going to be marrying the love of his life.

———

It was the next day when Mike eased himself into the warm water of the Japanese style hot tub and joined Ali on the submerged wooden bench. His fiancé wore a sleek black one piece that accented her luscious curves. They'd spent the day hiking, and now were taking a well-earned soak in a luxury outdoor spa overlooking the Shotover River.

"Mike, this place is heaven," she purred as he wrapped his muscular arms around her waist and manhandled her into the middle of the pool. He pressed his lips to hers and kissed her passionately as he caressed her chest.

"Easy boy," she murmured, sliding her hand down to his groin. "We've only got this tub for an hour."

"More than enough time," he slipped her breast from the bathing suit and kissed the nipple.

Ali slapped him playfully. "Is that right? You put a ring on my finger and the romance disappears?" She backed away from him adjusting her suit. Then with a wry grin she reached out and stabbed a button on the spa's control panel.

A cold stream of water shot out of an opening on the roof drilling him between the shoulder blades.

"Cool off, big boy."

Mike grunted and dropped underwater.

Ali turned off the water and waited for him to surface. A split second later she felt his hands on her hips. They worked their way up her stomach to her breasts and then his face emerged.

"So, cold water and frustration. Is that what I can expect as a married man?"

She kissed him again. "Of course. You knew that, right?"

Glancing over her shoulder he spotted a bright star above the mountains beyond the river. "Look, babe, first star I see tonight."

Turning she took two glasses of champagne from the tray next to the tub and handed one to him. "Make a wish and toast it."

He raised the glass then snuggled in behind her so they could both watch the horizon. "Life doesn't get any better than this."

"No it doesn't," she murmured.

They stared out at the darkening sky, watching as more stars appeared. It was Mike who broke the silence. "So, when do you want to get married?"

She shrugged. "I'm not picky. As long as the people I love are there, I'm happy. I vote for a low-key affair. No stress, just friends, family and Axe."

"I thought we could all hike up to Mount Otay and–"

"Stop right there. You're not turning this into some kind of military operation. I passed the Girlfriend Selection Course. No more shenanigans."

"Babe, I'm so over shenanigans."

She turned and kissed his cheek. "Me too. I don't even want a bachelorette party. Just a small ceremony."

"Well, then I'm not having a bachelor party."

"Mike, you can't do that to the boys. Rick will be heartbroken."

He sipped from his glass. "It's OK, I'll tell him it was your idea."

Ali snorted into hers. "You will not. They know we're engaged, right?"

"Um, well, TJ kinda does," he said, referring to his SEAL squad leader.

"You didn't tell them you were going to propose?" Ali reached out of the tub and found her phone. "We're going to tell them, now."

"Really, now?"

"Yes, I want to check on Axe." She dialed TJ and propped the phone against the bottle of champagne.

As the call connected they ducked down so only their faces were visible on the screen.

"Hello, Ali can you hear me?" TJ's voice came over the speaker, but the screen was pink. The camera was pointing into his ear.

"TJ, it's Mike. It's a video call. You need to take it away from your head."

The image changed to the inside of the squad's team room at Coronado in San Diego. They caught a glimpse of a shirtless heavily muscled African American seated on a weights bench, Rick the squad Corpsman. Then the camera revealed the craggy features of Chief 'TJ' Lines. "Hey, how are the lovebirds doing?"

"Is that Mike?" Rick bellowed in the background. A moment later he appeared alongside TJ. "Hi, Ali." Rick frowned. "Are you guys in a hot tub?"

"Yes, we've had a big day. How's my boy, Axe?" asked Ali.

"Hang on," said TJ as he moved the camera.

Axe, Mike's Military Working Dog was sitting in a chair staring at a cartoon playing on a laptop. Mike whistled and the Belgian Malinois snapped his head toward the screen. The top of his right ear flopped forward as he tilted his head.

"How's my beautiful boy?" gushed Ali.

Axe cocked his head the other way.

"He's so confused," Mike said with a laugh.

TJ appeared on the screen. "He's been a bit mopey, but apart from that he's good. The cartoons seem to help. So, what's news with you guys? Having a good time in Middle Earth?"

"It's been OK." Ali held up her hand so the Chief could see the engagement ring.

He squinted and then a broad grin split his craggy features. "Goddamn, that's fantastic news. Rick, our boy popped the question. Mike and Ali are getting married."

There was a clang as a dumbbell hit the ground. "Job well done, Frogman." Rick's face appeared. "Way to go and congratulations to you little lady." Then the expression on his face changed, as if a bolt of enlightenment had struck him. "Fuck yeah, this means we're gonna throw a bachelor party."

"Whoa there, Rick. Ali and I have decided to keep this real low key. A small ceremony and that's it."

TJ's face appeared. "Probably a good idea."

"What the fuck?" Rick exclaimed in the background. "That's so damn selfish."

TJ rolled his eyes. "OK, you kids enjoy the last few days of your vacation. We'll see you on Tuesday."

"Thanks, TJ. Pass on our best to Ernie and let him know the news," replied Ali.

They could still hear Rick ranting as the call terminated.

Ali kissed Mike's neck. "You think he'll be over it by the time we get back?"

He laughed. "Definitely not."

"I can't believe he's not going to have a bachelor party," Rick said as he hefted a dumbbell from the floor.

"Who's not having a bachelor party?" a short Latino asked as he entered the team room. Ernesto, or Ernie as his friends called him, was the SEAL squad's communications specialist. Together with Mike, Rick, TJ and Axe, they formed an elite fighting team.

"Mike, he and Ali are getting hitched," said Rick.

"Really, when did that happen?"

TJ ruffled Axe's ears. "Today, in New Zealand. He popped the big one and she said yes."

Ernie grinned. "That's fantastic news."

Rick dumped the weight on the floor. "Except the selfish bastard isn't having a bachelor party."

"What, that makes no sense. You can't get married without a bachelor party."

"Mike can," grumbled Rick.

"You ladies done?" snapped TJ. "You know bachelor parties were never meant to be tequila swilling strip fests.

The origin of the tradition stems from the Spartans, they held a feast to toast the groom and farewell his singlehood."

Rick yawned. "Boring. We need to take Mike to Tijuana and get him fuuuucked up."

TJ's eyes narrowed. "No. We need to take him on an epic adventure. Get him out in the woods away from the big smoke and back in touch with nature."

Rick shook his head and turned to Ernie. "You down with redneck shit or are you up for tequila and titties?"

The Latino's eyes narrowed. "Essé, I'm not going anywhere near Mexico with you. The Chief's idea sounds good. We get out in the woods. We drink a little bourbon around a fire and we chill."

"I've got a place in Willamette National Forest up in Oregon. We'll head up there for a weekend."

Rick sighed. "Great idea. Except for one thing, Mike and Ali have already laid down the law. No bachelor party."

TJ gave Axe another pat. "You leave that to me. In the meantime, we've got boats to clean."

Rick and Ernie let out a simultaneous groan.

"Why is it we only wash boats when Mike's away," moaned Rick.

TJ smiled. "Because I like him more than I like you."

Rick frowned. "You're supposed to like us all the same."

The Chief chuckled. "This is a SEAL team, not the goddamn Brady Bunch. Get your ass off that bench and get down to the sheds."

Chapter Three

Mike laughed as Axe let out an excited bark and danced around on the beach like a hyperactive puppy.

"I guess he missed you," said TJ with a chuckle as the team jogged along the beach.

"Wait till he sees Ali," said Mike as they reached the turnaround point and headed back toward the Navy base.

The four SEALs ran shirtless in the warm morning sun. Their bodies were covered in sand and salt from the rigorous training program the Chief had run to celebrate Mike's return. They'd started with pushups and crunches in the surf followed by a half mile swim and finally a three mile soft sand run.

Throughout the session Axe never left Mike's side. Over eighteen months had passed since the dog had been shot and thanks to Ali's veterinary skills he showed no sign of injury.

"So, how did the proposal go down?" asked TJ between breaths as they reached the end of their run.

Mike gave the boys a move-by-move breakdown of the entire operation as they stretched in a park.

"That's pretty slick essé," said Ernie when the story was complete.

"An operation that'd make any SEAL proud," added TJ.

"Not bad at all kid," said Rick. "Kicks all my proposals in the ass."

Mike frowned. "You've only been married once."

Rick shrugged. "I went through a phase of asking chicks to marry me. No big deal."

The other three men shared looks of disbelief.

"Anyway," he continued. "We need to talk about your bachelor party."

Mike grabbed a stick and tossed it across the park. Axe dashed after it. "Yeah, Ali and I are keen to keep this low key. We don't want a repeat of the Girlfriend Selection Course."

"You two wouldn't even be together if it wasn't for selection," said Rick. "Come on, brother. One last hit out with the team."

Axe dropped the stick at Mike's feet and looked up at him, tongue lolling from the side of his mouth. "One last hit out? I'm getting married not going to prison. The decision is final. No bachelor party."

"Does that mean you're not having a best man?" asked Ernie. "Because technically it was me who introduced you to Ali in the first place."

"The fuck! How you figure that?" snapped Rick.

"I recommended the vet. Even said she was pretty."

TJ finished stretching and sat on a bench seat. "That's true."

"Well, what about selection?" asked Rick.

"That was TJ's idea."

Rick frowned. "Yeah, well it was my element that let you SEAL the deal," he said accenting the words with his fingers.

Mike laughed. "Guys, I could never choose between you. You're all family. Plus, it was actually Axe who brought Ali and me together."

TJ grunted. "He's right, but you can't have a dog as your best man."

"True, and that's why I've asked my brother, Dean."

Rick frowned. "What the hell? I thought you were an only child?"

"That's because you're the world's worst listener. You're only interested in tits and ass," said Ernie.

"That's not true."

"Really? What's the Chief's wife's name?"

He frowned. "That's not fair. We never see her."

"Emily. Her name is Emily," answered Mike.

He shrugged. "I knew that."

TJ rose from the bench. "Rick, Mike and Ali want a low key event. We will respect that."

Rick scowled as he nodded. "Yeah, got it."

"Right," TJ continued. "Let's get back to work. We're running mask drills in the kill house."

Leonie's squeal of delight filled the café turning heads and earning a scowl from an elderly woman reading a paper. "Ali, it's freaking beautiful."

She blushed as her sister clutched her hand, inspecting the engagement ring.

"Holy shit! He must have dropped a bomb on this."

Her sister, a blonde middle-aged mother of two had a

real way with words. Ali's father always accused her of having a mouth dirtier than a railway worker's coveralls.

"And you said he proposed on a glacier with a violinist and a bottle of Dom?"

Ali smiled. "Yes, he did. It was the most romantic thing I've ever experienced."

"That's panty dropping right there. I'm wet just thinking about it."

She giggled. "Leonie!"

Her sister took a sip from her coffee. "That boy's a goddamn dreamboat." Her eyes shone as she smiled. "I am so happy for you." She lowered the cup to the table. "OK, so let's talk wedding. When you were little, you always wanted the whole nine yards: unicorns, carriages, doves, an orchestra and white lace. Yards and yards of white lace."

"Oh, that's right, I remember. No, Mike and I have agreed on a small intimate affair. I'm thinking one of the vineyards out near Swartz Canyon."

"Yes, with a string quartet and a reception under the vines. Big weddings are so passé."

"I knew you'd understand." She paused. "That's why you have to be my Maid of Honor."

Leonie smirked. "Please, who else could do the job?" She clapped her hands. "This is going to be so much fun. I am going to throw you the best bachelorette party this city has ever seen."

Ali scrunched up her face.

"What?"

"Mike and I kind of agreed we would keep things low key."

The happiness slid from Leonie's face. "You're kidding, right? No bachelorette party?"

Ali shook her head.

Her sister's jaw dropped. "Why would you do that? You know the bachelorette party isn't actually for you. It's for people like me. Ladies who haven't been drunk in months. Ladies who haven't felt the hot hard abs of an athlete since... Well, since ever."

"You're being a little dramatic."

"No, I'm not. You're entirely selfish." She folded her arms.

"OK, OK, maybe we can have a small gathering. Just a few girls, but it's not a party."

Leonie winked. "Got it. Let's call it pre-wedding drinks and..." She raised her hands and used her fingers as inverted commas. "Activities."

Ali frowned. "Minimal activities."

Her sister downed the last of her coffee. "Yeah, yeah whatever. OK babe, I've got to run." She leaned over and kissed Ali on the forehead. "I'm so happy for you. Give my best to Mike and Axe. I'll see you at the planning brunch on the weekend."

Ali drank the last of her latte as her sister left the café. She couldn't help but feel she was going to regret agreeing to a 'small' gathering. Still, Leonie was an amazing sister and a terrific mom to her nieces. If she needed to let down her hair a little who was Ali to say no?

The wedding planning team occupied a long table at Mike and Ali's favorite café, the Spanner Shop. The converted mechanic's garage was a short distance from her veterinary clinic and served the best coffee, sandwiches and muffins in a ten-mile radius.

Mike and Ali sat on one side of the table with TJ, Leonie and Mike's younger brother Dean, opposite.

The junior Saunders bore a close resemblance to his older brother. He had the same gray eyes, chiseled jaw and blonde hair. However, unlike his SEAL brother Dean had not followed their father into the services. He was a software engineer who spent most of his time perched behind a computer. As a result his hair reached his collar and he carried a little extra weight.

It was Mike who started the meeting. "Guys, firstly Ali and I would like to thank you for taking time out on a Saturday to help us wade through all this wedding stuff."

"You're the best," added Ali.

"It's also a chance for TJ, who's agreed to be the master of ceremonies, and Leonie, Ali's sister and maid of honor, to meet my brother and best man, Dean."

Leonie leaned across and whispered to Ali. "He's just as handsome and he's younger."

Ali shook her head and laughed as Mike continued. "I'm going to reemphasize that this is going to be a very low key event. About thirty guests and the bridal party."

"And a string quartet," added Leonie.

"Of course."

"Have you chosen a venue yet?" asked TJ.

Ali answered, "We've narrowed it down to three. Mike and I are heading out to Swartz Canyon after this to check them out." She glanced at her watch. "In fact, we're going to have to leave soon."

Leonie clapped her hands. "OK, venue aside we need to get to the most important part, the fashion. Ali, have you picked out a dress?"

"No, I thought you and I could do that next week."

"Lock it in. I'll get something to wear at the same time. Right, now for the boys."

"I thought I could wear dress uniform," said Mike.

TJ coughed into his fist. "Wear a tux."

Dean nodded in agreement. "Hey, bro. Proud of your service but this isn't about the military. This is for you and Ali."

Ali placed her hand on his. "I don't mind. It's up to you."

"Uniforms are sexy," added Leonie.

"Buy yourself a nice tuxedo. Every man should own one," TJ said. "Sure, get a few photos in your dress whites, but trust me, get married with class."

"Did you?" asked Mike.

TJ winked. "Damn straight I did. I wanted Emily to know she was marrying a man not a sailor. A man that would put her first over the service at the drop of a hat."

Mike nodded. "Tuxedo it is."

The Chief turned to Dean. "I've got an A-grade tailor that will sort both of you boys out. We'll hook it up for next week."

"Sounds good," replied Dean.

"Well that's the fashion," said Leonie. "Next we need to talk through decorations, music, invitations, food, gifts and timings. Oh, and most importantly, an engagement party."

Mike groaned.

Ali squeezed his hand. "Do we need an engagement party?"

Leonie shrugged. "Maybe not a party, just a sit-down dinner. I know Mom and Dad would love that."

Ali nodded. "OK, can you come up with some options? Mike and I need to get going."

They rose from the table and Ali hugged everyone.

Then the pair disappeared out the front door leaving TJ, Dean and Leonie at the table.

"A buddy of mine owns a restaurant in town. Mike took Ali there on one of their first dates so it might be a good venue," said TJ.

"Just 'n' Thyme?" asked Leonie.

"That's the one."

She rolled her eyes. "It took me three months to get a table."

"Yeah, he tells me it's doing well. I'll make a call and let you know, but right now we get down to the real business."

"Which is?" asked Dean.

"The bachelor and bachelorette party."

Leonie's eyes lit up. "Oh hell yeah. Tell me more, Mr. SEAL."

Chapter Four

TJ's buddy had insisted on closing one of his dining rooms to host Mike and Ali's engagement dinner at his restaurant, Just 'n' Thyme. Thirty-five of their closest friends and family joined them in the romantic setting. Ali's parents had flown in from Nebraska, Mike's mom had come down from San Jose, and of course the team was in attendance along with their Commanding Officer.

The meal was a sumptuous three-course affair that started with oysters, progressed to lobster and rack of lamb, before concluding with a delicate adaptation of the classic, tiramisu.

When dinner was finished, Mike rose and thanked everyone for attending. He quickly told an abridged version of the proposal and professed his undying love for Ali. She added a few words of her own before they handed over to TJ, the master of ceremonies.

"Ladies and gentlemen, firstly I want to thank my old friend James for putting on a fabulous dinner." He gestured to the owner who was standing in the corner.

The room broke into applause.

He waited for silence then continued. "Most of you, if not all, are aware of the events that brought Ali and Mike together. One very special dog, who unfortunately couldn't be here tonight, but sends his regards, plus a series of challenges that myself and two other people in this room may or may not have played a role in concocting."

There was nervous laughter from Rick and Ernie's table.

"Needless to say, Ali came through. Not only for Mike and Axe but also Rick, Ernie and myself. In fact, we, like Axe, owe her our lives." He raised his glass. "Ladies and gentlemen, I'd like you to be upstanding."

The room rose and lifted their glasses.

"To Ali, a beautiful person and a killer teammate."

The room echoed his toast.

"Now, before we wrap up I would like to present a small gift to Ali and Mike from the rest of the team. It's not much, but it may go a small way to make up for the trauma of the Girlfriend Selection Course." He took an envelope from under his jacket and handed it to Ali. "You kids have a great time."

Later that night, in the townhouse he shared with Ali, Mike measured a scoop of dog food and emptied it into Axe's bowl. The hound looked up at him with a furrowed brow. "OK, fine." He sighed and added another half scoop to the bowl. "Don't blame me if you start getting fat."

Axe let out an excited bark and started eating.

Mike washed his hands and left the kitchen.

"Mike, you have to see this," Ali's voice sounded from the bedroom.

He pushed open the door to find his fiancé sitting on the bed in sleek satin underwear. She had an envelope in her hands and a smile on her face.

Mike stood in the doorway a moment and ran his eyes over her voluptuous body. Damn she was sexy.

"The boys got us a weekend away in a five-star resort in Oregon."

Mike removed his shirt and hung it on a chair. "They have resorts in Oregon?"

Ali nodded as she flicked through a pamphlet. "Yes and it looks amazing. It's got a day spa, restaurant, golf course, horses and it's set in the most beautiful forest." She held up a handwritten note. "And TJ knows the manager so we can take Axe."

"Of course he does. TJ knows everyone." Mike tossed his pants over his shirt, lowered himself onto the bed and slid toward her. "Sounds too good to be true. What's the catch?" He kissed her stomach.

"They booked us tickets. It's the weekend before the wedding."

He worked his way up her body to her cleavage. "Isn't that a bad time to go?" he murmured.

She moaned softly. "No, everything should be arranged by then. It's going to be the perfect time to relax."

"Sounds great." He kissed her neck and then nibbled her ear.

Her hands traced their way down his hard body as he reached under and unsnapped her bra with a deft touch. Their lips met as she reached down and squeezed gently. "We're going to have the best time."

"Now or at the resort?"

"Both."

Chapter Five

Rick drummed his fingers on the steering wheel as he drove Ernie's minivan through Las Vegas on Interstate 15. He shook his head as the black-glass pyramid of the The Luxor Hotel flashed past. "This is the cruelest shit I've ever heard of. Driving through Vegas to get to a redneck bachelor party in the mountains. That's ruthless as fuck, TJ."

In the passenger seat the Chief looked up from the book he was reading. "Trust me, it's the best way."

Rick glanced up at a huge sign announcing the Bellagio Hotel. "Come on. We're here. Surely we can stop overnight. Maybe catch a show at the Spearmint Rhino."

TJ shook his head. "Negative, we need to be in Fallon by lunchtime."

Rick glanced in the rear-view mirror. The other two passengers, Dean and Ernie were fast asleep. "Is that where we're changing teams?"

"Yeah, why? You getting tired?"

He yawned. "A little." Rick had been driving since they left San Diego five hours earlier.

"OK, pull into the next gas station and we'll grab some coffee and switch."

Twenty minutes later Rick sat in the passenger seat with a can of energy drink in one hand and his phone in the other. TJ was now behind the wheel, and Dean and Ernie were awake.

"Are you kidding me?" Rick exclaimed as he stared at the phone.

"What's wrong? Already run out of Tinder matches?" asked Dean.

"No, worse. There are literally zero strippers within a hundred miles of Oakridge, Oregon."

"Oh no, essé. What are you going to do? You might have to dress up and give Mike a lap dance," said Ernie.

"You'd like that, wouldn't you? You sick little midget."

"No need to get racist," replied the Latino.

"What, how is midget racist?"

"You were implying that Mexicans are much shorter than black men."

Rick turned with a cocked eyebrow. "Brother, you've got a serious complex." Returning his attention to his phone he missed the wink that Ernie shot Dean.

"OK, looks like your crappy little town has a pole dancing studio. That's pretty much stripping, right?"

TJ shook his head. "It used to be such a quaint place."

"Is that where you grew up?" asked Ernie as Rick thumbed an email on his phone.

"No, used to visit a lot. My grandfather built the cabin when I was a kid. We'd head up there most summers. Swim in the lake, raft the river and hunt deer. Some of my best times were had in those mountains."

Rick continued on his phone.

"What about you, Dean?" asked TJ. "You and Mike get out in the wilderness much?"

He nodded. "Yeah, we grew up on Navy bases though, so we spent more time in the water. The old man was posted to Pearl for a few years. We got up in the mountains there a fair bit."

"Mike doesn't talk much about his dad," said Ernie.

Dean nodded. "When dad died he took it pretty hard. They were real close. Mike idolized him. I was always closer to mom."

"Jackpot!" Rick punched his fist in the air.

"Tinder match?" asked Dean.

"Better, we've got ourselves a pole dancer for tomorrow night."

"You could turn a nun's picnic into a gangbang, couldn't you Rick?" growled TJ.

He grinned. "What can I say, it's a gift."

Ali's face was glued to the window of their hired sedan as it turned off the highway and entered the McCredie Springs Country Club. "Oh Mike, it's beautiful," she exclaimed as he drove them along a tree-lined laneway. They'd flown up from San Diego mid-afternoon and driven the sixty miles from the city of Eugene to their destination.

Mike parked the car in front of a grand southern-style mansion. As they stepped outside a man in his fifties dressed in jeans, boots and a McCredie Springs embroidered shirt appeared from inside.

"You must be Mike and Ali," he declared in a deep voice.

"That's us." Mike shook his hand. "Oh, and we've got Axe in the back."

"The hero, right?"

Ali smiled. "The one and only. Thank you so much for letting us bring him along."

"Hey, it's no problem at all. We've got a villa set aside for people with dogs. My name's Brian and if there's anything you need, you let me know."

"Thanks, Brian. I tell you what, this has to be the prettiest place I've ever seen," said Ali.

"We try. Now, I'll show you to your villa. The boys will bring your luggage along momentarily. Mike, if you leave your keys in the car, they'll park it for you and drop them off with the bags."

They let Axe out of the sedan and followed Brian down a stone pathway that weaved between tall birch trees. Birds flitted among the branches, their calls filling the air.

"You're welcome to let Axe run in the forest. However, we've got horses in the bottom paddock. They're fine with dogs, but Axe might not like them." He gestured to a velvet smooth green. "Mike are you much of a golfer?"

"I certainly am."

"Good, because I find that nine holes take about the same time as the deluxe spa treatment. Which, I might add is included with your room."

Ali grasped his arm. "You mean you won't be joining me?"

Mike laughed. "Hey, someone has to look after Axe."

She kissed his cheek. "So that's why you wanted to bring him."

They reached a quaint weatherboard cottage perched in the woods. Two stories with a deck it was framed with vine-laden trellis. As they climbed the steps to the porch Ali spotted a hot tub nestled in the garden.

"Mike, this is the best."

Brian swiped an electronic lock and pushed open the bi-fold doors revealing an opulent living area. There was a kitchen, dining setting, couches and a chandelier hanging from the ceiling.

"There are two bedrooms upstairs, both with their own bathrooms." He reached out and ruffled Axe's ears. "If you need anything just holler." He slipped away outside leaving the three of them alone.

"The boys have outdone themselves," said Ali as she climbed the stairs to the second floor.

Mike followed her and Axe upstairs. "The selection fiasco didn't exactly set the bar high."

"OK, now this is nice," announced Ali.

The master bedroom opened up onto a balcony with views out over the valley. White gauze curtains danced in the breeze. He turned around and was confronted by a dazzling white bathroom with an enormous brass-footed bathtub.

Ali was standing in front of it smiling. "I think we're going to be very comfortable here." She frowned and nodded toward the bed.

Mike looked over and saw Axe sprawled on the duvet. "Someone already is. Axe, off."

The dog jumped down and disappeared downstairs.

He turned back to Ali as she slipped her summer dress's shoulder straps off and let it drop to the floor. Beneath it, she wore lacy white underwear. She pouted her lips and pointed to his pants. "Mike, off."

It was early morning when TJ parked the van in front of a log cabin nestled among the trees on the shore of a lake. He stepped out, took a few paces, lifted his arms wide and sucked in a lungful of crisp mountain air.

The other three occupants of the van were a little slower to gather themselves. Dean and Ernie climbed out of the back of the van and stretched. Rick continued slumbering in the front passenger seat.

TJ opened his door. "Rise and shine cupcake, it's time to get this place ready for action."

Rick opened one eye. "You sir, are an asshole."

The boys unloaded their bags and boxes of supplies as TJ unlocked the cabin. He swung open the door and childhood memories came flooding back. The bunkhouse was exactly how he remembered it. It consisted of a single open room with bunks across the back and a massive fireplace at one end. At the other was the kitchen with its lake facing windows and an old cast iron cooker.

"Wow!" Rick let out a low whistle as he entered carrying a carton of Bulleit Bourbon. "Hey Pops, you shoot that?" He placed the booze on a rough-hewn table in the center of the cabin and gestured to a stuffed black bear in the corner of the room.

TJ shook his head. "Nope, grandma killed that one with her bare hands."

Rick frowned.

"Chief, this is a pretty special place," said Ernie as he and Dean entered with cartons of food.

"Yeah, man. Thanks for bringing us up here," added Dean.

"My pleasure, boys. Right, Rick, you check the raft. Should be in the boatshed. Dean, you get those rations stowed." He pointed to the shelves in the kitchen. "Ernie, lay the map on the table. I'll fire up the stove and get some coffee on. Full mission briefing in fifteen."

The men snapped into action like a well-oiled machine. Exactly fifteen minutes later with mugs of coffee in hand they gathered around the map that Ernie had pinned to the table.

"OK boys, we're here." TJ used the tip of a bowie knife to show their location. "Eugene city is over here." He pointed off the map. "McCredie Springs is here." He tapped the tip on the edge of the National Forest. "And the river is here." He traced a thin blue line that ran through the middle of the forest from north to south.

"Looks pretty remote," observed Ernie.

"It is. Twenty-two miles of untouched wilderness."

Rick unscrewed a bottle of bourbon and sloshed it in his coffee. "We're taking guns, right?"

"We're on the river. What are you going to shoot, fish?"

"The guns are for protection. Haven't you seen Deliverance?" Rick exposed his teeth in his best impersonation of a hick. "Hey boy, you squeal like a pig?"

TJ rolled his eyes. "This is Oregon, not West Virginia."

"Same shit. We need guns."

TJ tapped the bourbon bottle with his blade. "You going to be sober at any stage of this activity?"

Rick considered his point. "Nope."

"Then no guns." The Chief checked his watch. "I need to be at the airport in two and a half hours. I'll drop you boys at McCredie on the way through. You get eyes on the target and when I get back we'll make the snatch."

Rick raised his hand. "Question."

"Shoot."

"Can I stay here and get things ready for tonight?"

"Sure, but don't wander off into the woods. The bears are pretty active this time of year."

"Bears? What the fuck TJ, what hellhole have you brought us to? This is supposed to be a bachelor party not the god damn hunger games."

TJ spun the Bowie knife in his palm and flicked it into the wood. "Rick, stop being such a pansy, you'll be fine." He gestured to the others. "Get your gear sorted. We roll in thirty."

Leonie grabbed her bags from an airport conveyor belt and joined the women waiting at the exit. It was nine in the morning and they'd caught the first flight up from San Diego. As maid of honor she was responsible for the group of six. The bachelorette party consisted of two of Ali's friends from college, her assistant Naomi, a girl she played tennis with and Ernie's wife, Maria.

"OK ladies, is everyone ready?"

They let out a resounding cheer and Leonie led them out of the arrivals lounge. She spotted TJ standing alongside a minivan. She waved and he strode over.

She gave his cargo pants, checked shirt and baseball cap a once over. "Look at you, all rugged and outdoorsy."

He frowned at her bulging bags. "You do know you're only here for two nights."

"It's not all for me. I've packed vital party supplies."

He let out a grunt as he lifted the bags. "Lead pipes?" Lowering them into the trunk he slammed it shut. "We've got a little over an hours drive. There's a liquor store on the way. Is there anything else you ladies need before we reach the resort?"

Leonie glanced around the group. Everyone looked to her expectantly. "Sounds good."

The girls clambered aboard and soon they were on the highway heading south.

"So how come Mrs. Chief wasn't available for this little foray?" asked Leonie from the passenger seat.

"Emily was keen, but she's away on a business trip."

"Ah, that sucks. What line of work is she in?"

"She's a food critic."

"Get out of town."

TJ laughed. "What, too civilized for a sailor?"

"No, just not what I expected."

"I was a chef before I joined up."

"Do you clean as well?"

"Huh, I guess so. Why?"

"It's the ultimate package. Cooks, kills and cleans. You're Casey goddamn Ryback." Leonie reached into her handbag and removed a hip flask. "OK ladies, let's get this party started."

The van filled with laughter and TJ shook his head. He pressed the accelerator a little harder. The sooner he got to McCredie the sooner he could offload the six women.

Chapter Six

Mike tipped his head and cracked his neck before adjusting his stance and grip on a golf club. He drew back the five iron and drove through the ball.

"Oh yeah," he murmured as it sailed down the fairway and bounced toward the green. "You see that?" He turned to where Axe was lying on the grass chewing a bone. "Nailed it." The dog paid him no attention. "Yeah, I thought as much."

He returned the club to his bag and grabbed the handle. "OK, buddy. Let's roll."

Axe picked up his bone and trotted down the fairway alongside him. Mike checked his watch and smiled. He had enough time for a few more holes before meeting Ali at the villa. His thoughts turned to the wedding and how simple Ali was making the whole process. He had literally been to a coffee date, the engagement dinner and a suit fitting. In fact, everyone including his SEAL squad were being super helpful. Hell, he was getting married next week and here he was strolling along a fairway at a five-star resort with his best friend; life was good.

He reached his ball, selected a pitching wedge and lined up. The green was beyond a small rise. He could barely see the top of the flag. Chipping high he watched with satisfaction as the shot sailed toward the pin.

Axe chewed his bone as Mike scanned the green for the ball. There was no sign of it. Hoping for a birdie, he checked the hole; no ball. "You're kidding me," he mumbled, searching the grass at the edge of the green. He made his way into the undergrowth. Axe joined him as he poked in the pine needles.

The dog gave a bark and disappeared into the bushes with his tail wagging. "You found it?" he asked, following.

"Looking for this?" Ernie's voice startled him as he pushed through branches and saw his teammate holding the ball. Axe jumped up and licked the Latino's face.

Mike frowned. "What the hell are you doing here?"

"I'm here for the party."

There was a rustle to Mike's flank and TJ appeared holding a pair of plasticuffs. "We can do this the easy way or the hard way."

There was another noise to his right and Dean emerged clutching a black hood.

Mike glanced down at Axe who was sitting with his tongue lolling from his mouth. "Are you kidding me? You're not even going to try and protect me?"

The dog cocked his head and his ear flopped forward.

"Does Ali know about this?" Mike asked as he handed his club to Ernie and held his wrists together.

Dean slid the hood over his head as TJ cuffed him.

"By now she's got problems of her own," TJ replied with a laugh.

"Seriously, if this involves cartel hit men I'm going to be pissed."

Ali felt amazing. Her skin had never felt smoother in her life. Three hours of pampering at the day spa had been exactly what she needed. The planning for the wedding hadn't been particularly stressful. Leonie and TJ had taken care of most of the details, but it was still good to relax in the hands of a talented masseuse.

She strolled along the path to the villa enjoying the sunshine and the warm breeze on her face. Stepping onto the porch, she spotted Mike's golf clubs and smiled. He would have enough time to enjoy her smooth body before dinner.

Axe greeted her at the stairs and she stopped to pat him. Her smile widened as she spotted the drawn curtains. It looked as if Mike had something similar in mind.

Pushing open the doors she ducked through the gossamer material. "Mike, babe, I feel fantastic!"

"Surprise!" The screams of six female voices nearly sent her diving back outside. Leonie stood at the front of the pack with a huge cocktail glass in her hand. She thrust the beverage and its penis-shaped straw toward Ali.

"Welcome to your bachelorette party, little sister."

She gave the villa an uneasy scan, noting the phallic-themed decorations strung across the ceiling. Rows of alcohol bottles and cocktail glasses filled the kitchen bench top. Then it dawned on her. The resort and the day spa were all an elaborate plan.

She smiled, took a slurp from the cocktail and winced at the taste of tequila. "You are so devious."

The girls circled her lifting their glasses in the air. Axe joined them jumping up and down with excitement as they whooped and hollered.

"So what's the plan?" asked Ali. "What happened to Mike? I'm guessing the boys grabbed him?"

Leonie topped up her cocktail. "Correct, we're meeting up with them tomorrow afternoon. However, till then we're going to party like it's 1999."

Maria, Ernie's wife, joined them. The short buxom Mexican hugged Ali and planted a kiss on her cheek. "Tonight we've got a beautiful dinner. Then your sister can continue with her depraved plans."

Leonie shrugged. "She insisted."

Ali smiled. "Maria, I am so glad you're here to add a touch of class."

Her sister laughed. "Class? Sweetheart, we're drinking from cock straws."

The villa filled with laughter and Ali grinned. Maybe a bachelorette party wasn't such a bad idea after all.

Mike felt the van come to a halt and heard the door slide open. He was bundled outside and then the hood was ripped off. He'd guessed they were on their way to TJ's cabin and he was correct.

The Chief released the cuffs from Mike's wrists. "Welcome to paradise."

"TJ, this is great," he exclaimed, examining the rough-hewn log building.

"Yeah, been in the family a long time."

At that moment the cabin door swung open and Rick

appeared on the deck with a glass in each hand. "Mikey boy, welcome to the last day of your FREEEEEEDOM!"

Mike laughed. "Rick, are you already wasted?"

The African American embraced him in a hug. "Not yet, but the night is young. Fellas, come inside, I've got someone I want you to meet."

"Here we go," said TJ as Dean and Ernie followed him into the cabin.

In the few hours that they'd been gone Rick had made some minor adjustments to the interior layout. The kitchen table had been moved to the far end of the room and served as a well-stocked bar. The couches had been shoved into each corner and the open space was now occupied by what looked like half a dozen stripper poles.

In front of the fireplace Mike spotted a tall woman dressed in leggings and a crop top. She had the body of a dancer and a girl next door face that was painted with a broad smile.

She waved at them. "Hi guys, my name's Jenny. Are you ready to get started?"

TJ turned to Rick. "What the hell's going on here?"

Rick shrugged. "It would seem that pole dancing is not the same as stripping." He downed one of his drinks and gestured to the bar. "Let's give it a go."

Mike doubled over with laughter. "Rick, you're a champion." He poured himself a bourbon and downed it. "Come on boys, let's get into it." He moved across and grabbed a pole. "Right, Jenny, I'm Mike. Exactly how do we do this?"

The staff at the Country Club had set aside a private dining area for the girls. The room was decorated with bouquets of white flowers, the tables laid with crisp linen and fine silver cutlery. Classical music played from a stereo in the corner as the women enjoyed an exceptional dining experience.

Ali, dressed in an elegant lace dress sat at the head of the table with a plastic tiara perched on her head. The other women, equally as resplendent, sat around her.

As dessert was served Leonie interrupted the conversation by striking her champagne glass with the back of the knife. It subsequently shattered unleashing its contents on the table. "Oh, fuck."

The girls broke into laughter as Maria used her napkin to abate the tidal wave of sparkling white.

Leonie tapped the stem of the shattered glass. "OK ladies, calm down. As usual, Maria has it under control." She paused as the girls clapped. "I'd like to take the opportunity to thank her for organizing this beautiful dinner."

The girls all cheered.

"Now, we all know that my baby sister is the reason we're here. Next week she marries a guy who may well be the sweetest dreamboat in the history of single men. And God knows after the dick weeds she's dated, she deserves him."

Ali smiled. "Thanks, sis."

"But, married is next week. Tonight she's going to party hard." Leonie nodded to a girl positioned next to the stereo system. "So ladies, I hope you've left enough room for another round of dessert, because here come the sweetest treats you've ever seen."

Classical music was suddenly replaced by a thumping beat and the doors to the dining room burst open. At first, no one appeared. Then, as the music peaked, two handsome twenty-something men dressed as a fireman and police officer strutted into view.

"Woo, hoo. Happy bachelorette Ali!" screamed Leonie as the strippers danced their way into the room and circled the ladies like hungry sharks.

Ali blushed as they made their way to the head of the table and danced suggestively on either side of her. The fireman was the first to disrobe, letting his jacket fall to reveal a rock hard body.

The girls whooped and cheered as the police officer followed his cue and ripped open his shirt. The scantily clad men took it in turns to rub their sculpted torsos on either side of Ali. She giggled, trying hard not to burst into laughter as they took her hands and traced them over their abs.

"Leonie, you're so dead," she mouthed.

Her sister raised a fresh glass. "Live it up baby, this is your night."

***

Meanwhile, less than twenty miles away the boy's night was progressing somewhat differently. Mike, TJ, Dean and Ernie had abandoned their attempts at pole dancing and had resorted to drinking as they watched an inebriated Rick try to follow Jenny's instructions.

"OK, Rick. Let's move to something more advanced." Jenny hauled herself up the pole, flipped upside down, wrapped her legs around it, released her hands and slowly spun around the pole to the ground.

Perched on a stool, TJ poured himself another bourbon. "You're pushing shit uphill, Jenny. That big ox will never be able to do that." He turned to Mike and winked.

"What the hell, granddad. I don't see any other mother-fucker out here trying this pole shit." Rick stripped to his briefs revealing muscles that would put a professional athlete to shame.

"And the fish takes the bait," said Ernie.

Mike laughed. "Every time."

Rick hauled himself effortlessly up the pole, flipped upside down and wrapped his legs around it.

"I just realized why you're so good at this," said TJ.

"Because I'm strong," yelled Rick as he contemplated releasing his hands.

"No, because you're the only one who shaves his legs. It's a matter of friction."

Mike snickered into his drink and bourbon shot from his nose. He hunched over coughing as the others burst into laughter.

"Serves you right, bachelor boy. Should be you up this damn pole," yelled Rick from where he was hanging.

Standing in the corner, Jenny suppressed a smirk. "Come on Rick, they all gave up. You can do this."

"Damn straight I can. I'm a frogman." He released the pole and slowly spun around it toward the ground.

"He's actually doing it," yelled Dean. "He's actually doing it."

Ernie started the chant. "Rick, Rick, Rick."

In a matter of seconds everyone, including Jenny was yelling the pole dancing Navy SEAL's name.

Then, as he got closer to the ground he started gathering speed. Then he lost traction and dropped like a rock, landing on his head with a thump. His legs unlatched from the pole and he collapsed into a motionless heap.

The room fell silent.

Suddenly Rick jumped to his feet. "Nailed it!" He

sprinted across to Mike, snatched his drink, downed it and grabbed the bachelor in a bear hug. "I did it for you, Mikey, because soon you're going to be locked in the prison of monogamy."

TJ slapped him on the shoulder. "Way to go, bud."

Jenny joined them at the makeshift bar. "That was pretty good. I've got girls I've been training for months who can't pull off that move."

Rick turned to face her. "That's because they're not SEALs."

She met his gaze and then lowered her eyes slowly over his body. "No, they're most definitely not." Then she looked away. "OK, well things look like they're going to get pretty messy here. So, I'm going to leave you to it."

Rick frowned. "You sure we can't convince you to take off–"

Jenny silenced him with a raised finger. "You were doing so good, pretty boy. Now help me pack these poles."

Mike suppressed a grin as Rick helped her pack the equipment.

"Well I'll be damned," said TJ. "I ain't ever seen a lady put that boy in his place."

"Must have been the bump to the head. He's gone all loco," added Ernie.

"Right, show's over." Dean took a pack of cards from his pocket. "Do you guys know how to play asshole?"

Mike snorted. "Hell yeah, we do. We're the guys it's named after."

TJ pulled a box of cigars from a drawer. "Dean, you smoke?"

"Cubans or reefers?"

The Chief's eyes narrowed.

"I was joking. Cubans are cool."

As Dean dealt the cards Rick carried the bags containing Jenny's poles out of the cabin. He placed them at the back of her car and quickly ducked into the bushes to pee while she went in to say goodbye to the team.

As he relieved himself he heard something rustling in the bushes. Squinting he tried to identify the source. There was a loud growl and he caught a glimpse of long white fangs in the moonlight. Zipping his fly, he backed away then turned and ran. As he burst from the bushes he almost collided with Jenny.

"Bear! There's a bear," he whispered.

She smiled. "Really, where?"

Rick turned and pointed. The animal lumbered out of the bushes, saw Jenny and rocked back on its haunches. In the glow of the cabin's lights he could see its teeth. It seemed to be eyeing him hungrily.

Jenny fumbled in her bag and pulled out a flashlight. She shone it on the bear's face. The animal let out a low growl.

"Don't do that. You're making it angry."

She shook her head. "She's tagged. I know this bear." Jenny put the flashlight away, clapped her hands and took a step toward the beast. It reared up to its full height. "Off you go, Nancy. Stop being a little trash pig."

The bear let out a grumble then turned and disappeared into the bushes.

Jenny unlocked her car. "If she comes around again make some loud noises and chase her off. This time of year they're looking for easy food. Trust me, she's more scared than you."

Rick managed a weak nod.

"Was nice meeting you all. I might see you around the

park." She climbed inside, started the car and drove off, leaving Rick standing in the dark.

"Hey pole dancer," bellowed Ernie. "You going to stay out there moping or you going to join the party?"

"Yeah, coming." Rick climbed the stairs and took the drink Ernie offered him. "What did I miss?"

"We're playing asshole and Mike's winning."

Rick cracked his knuckles. "Well, it's time to turn that around. Let's get this pretty boy bachelor messed up."

Chapter Seven

Rick lay on a patch of sun-soaked grass. He was dressed in a full-length wetsuit, buoyancy vest, backpack and a helmet. Mike and Dean, dressed in a similar fashion, sat on a log a few feet away. All three were nursing monster hangovers.

A dozen yards away on the bank of a river TJ was lashing a cooler to the center of a blue inflatable raft. Ernie sat on the side of the rubber boat, using a foot pump to inflate it.

"What the hell did I drink last night?" asked Rick. "My head feels like I landed on it."

Dean laughed. "That's because you did. You don't remember the pole incident?"

He sat up. "No, but I do remember a bear and a beautiful woman."

Mike sighed. "Jenny, the pole dancing instructor. I don't remember any bears."

"There was one outside. She chased it away. The woman is goddamn Tarzan." He stretched out his arms and lay down. "I think I'm in love."

TJ tossed a paddle and it landed on his chest. "You fall in love every week. Now, everyone get your asses on the raft."

The three hungover men rose to their feet and walked slowly to the boat.

"All hands on," ordered TJ once Ernie had the pump stowed. They grabbed a handle each.

"Prepare to lift, lift."

They heaved the boat up and slid it across the rocky bank into the river. TJ took the back right spot as the others clambered in. Rick positioned himself in the center alongside the cooler.

"Y'all know how this works?" asked TJ as he guided the raft toward the middle of the river.

Dean shook his head.

"Pretty simple. I'll tell you when and what direction to paddle. Try to stay in the boat. If you get thrown out go feet first through the rapids and then swim to the raft. We'll pull you back in or meet up with you on the other side. Don't swim toward large rocks. They're bad news."

The men nodded in unison.

"We've got a half-dozen smaller rapids before we hit the big stuff. So you better get your shit together. Rick, you might want to join the rest of us on the tubes."

Rick waved his hand. "I'm good."

"OK, suit yourself. Right, forward paddle."

The splash of the water, warmth of the sun and comfort of the rubber raft soon lulled Rick into a slumber. He faintly registered the roar of water rushing over rocks as they progressed downstream.

"Back paddle!"

TJ's yell woke him and he opened his eyes, raising his

head to see what was going on. As he did the raft bucked under him.

"What the fuck?" he bellowed as he fell and bounced off the ice chest.

"Woo hoo! Hell yeah," yelled Mike as he rode the raft like a bucking bronco.

Rick struggled to his knees as they hit the next rapids. He looked up and caught a wink from TJ.

"See you later, bud."

He lunged for one of the rope handles as the raft bucked again throwing him head first over the side. Ice-cold water drove the air from his lungs. A rock smacked his hip as he fought his way to the surface and sucked in a breath of air. Then he shot head first over a small waterfall.

Suddenly he felt like he was in a washing machine. Surrounded by foaming white water he was tumbled like dirty laundry. Right as he was starting to panic the hydraulic action released him, spitting him back into the river.

Gasping for breath he looked downstream, searching for the raft. He spotted it a dozen yards away. Concerned faces scanned the river for him.

"There he is!" yelled Dean as Rick swam toward them.

TJ held a paddle out and he grabbed it, dragging him toward the boat. "Got yourself a solid recirculation there, buddy." The Chief chuckled as the team hauled him into the raft.

"God damn!" bellowed Rick. "Now I'm awake."

Laughter echoed off the water as he grabbed his paddle and joined the others, sitting on the edge of the raft.

"Did it clear your hangover?" asked Dean.

"Hell yeah, it did."

Mike's brother grinned. "Good, then I'm going in on the next one."

"There's a soft set coming up. You can swim them safely. I wouldn't recommend hitting a grade three like Rick."

"You could have warned me."

"Pretty sure I did."

The next mile of rafting went smoothly with the boys taking it in turns to slip from the craft and ride the white water, except TJ who stayed at the helm. Soon they were past the first series of rapids and floating gently downstream.

"Anyone else sore from that pole dancing?" asked Dean as they cruised through a pristine stretch of forest.

Rick cracked his neck. "I'm the only one who should be sore. The rest of you pansies skipped out soon as it got tough."

"We're not as streamlined as you," said Ernie. "My package was getting in the way."

"Yeah and we weren't trying to impress Jennifer," said Mike.

"Trying? Please, she loved my action," replied Rick.

"Is that before or after she had to save you from the scary bear?" asked TJ.

"There was a bear!"

"I don't doubt it. The woods are full of them, but they're completely harmless and terrified of people."

Rick scowled. "That's not true. Grizzly bears eat people all the time."

"That may well be, but there ain't no grizzlies in these woods, only black bears. And they're not dangerous."

"Yeah, well when you've got your Johnson out anything with teeth is a threat."

"That's a fair point," said Dean.

As they cruised slowly around a curve in the river the dull roar of more rapids reached their ears.

"Time to stop thinking about broads 'n' bears and focus," barked TJ. "This is our first set of grade four rapids. Stand by for my command."

———

The smell of eggs and bacon assaulted Ali's nose, waking her from a drunken slumber. She stretched out in the crisp white sheets of her king sized bed and let out a groan. The aroma of coffee wafted through the bedroom and her stomach rumbled.

As she sat up her head throbbed. She reached for a glass of water from her nightstand and tipped it down her parched throat.

Then she heard claws rattling on the wooden floor and a damp nose snuffled its way over the edge of the bed into her hand.

"Morning, Axe," she croaked as she stepped out of bed and wrapped herself in a robe.

Stumbling downstairs she found Maria in the kitchen. She greeted Ali with a vibrant smile. "Good morning. How are you feeling?"

Ali sat on a stool and leaned on the counter. "Terrible."

Maria placed a mug in front of her and poured piping hot coffee into it. "Well, that's what happens when you drink too much, but it's OK. Aunty Maria will sort you out."

Ali smiled and sipped the coffee. "What are you making?"

"Mexican omelets. I make them every time Ernie goes out drinking. Chases a hangover straight out the door." She returned to the stove and checked a frying pan. "Almost ready."

Axe placed his head on Ali's knee and she ruffled his ears. "So, what's on the cards today?"

"Today we have a girly day. Day spa, high tea and then a picnic dinner at the river with the boys."

"That sounds perfect."

Maria tipped an omelet onto a plate and slid it in front of Ali. "You eat this, and I'll go and wake the others." She removed her apron and left the villa.

Ali took a bite of the omelet. It tasted incredible. Sipping more coffee, her thoughts turned to Mike. According to Leonie, the boys were spending the day white water rafting. She grimaced, she couldn't think of anything worse than paddling with a hangover. Nope, a day spa and high tea sounded far more civilized.

***

"Paddle hard, boys!" TJ bellowed as he steered the raft around a massive boulder and down a narrow chute.

The team hollered with excitement as the raft bounced over rocks, surging through the white water into a fast flowing channel.

"Hell yeah. That was wicked," announced Rick as their speed subsided.

"Not a bad way to spend the day," agreed Mike.

"Better than Vegas strippers?" asked Ernie as TJ directed the raft toward the bank.

Rick dipped his paddle propelling them forward. "Let's not get too excited."

"OK boys, paddle hard." TJ aimed the nose of the raft at a pebbled beach.

The team dug deep, propelling the craft out of the

current and onto the bank. Ernie leaped from the front, grabbed a rope and tied it off to a log.

"Let's have some lunch," said TJ as they carried the cooler ashore.

Fifteen minutes later the Chief had a fire roaring under a skillet layed with minute steak. The cooler was open and Ernie was hard at work slicing tomato, cheese and pickles. Rick, Mike and Dean had positioned themselves on a log with beers in hand.

"Yeah, this is the life," said Rick. "I could get used to this. Get me a little cabin and invite Jenny around for some dancing, drinking and loving."

"You'd want her around all the time if you lived out here," said Mike.

"Hell yeah, she is one sexy lady."

"No, I mean to save you from the scary bears."

The boys broke into laughter.

Rick shook his head. "I knew I shouldn't have told you."

"It's OK essé," added Ernie. "We all know you can't 'bear' to keep a secret."

More laughter filled the beach.

TJ rose from the fire with the skillet in hand. "OK boys, meat's up."

The log served as a table as they lined up with beers in one hand and rolls in the other. They sandwiched the tender beef in crusty bread, layering it with relish, pickles, cheese and tomatoes.

"This is real good, TJ," complimented Dean. "What's the meat?"

"Venison shot in these very mountains."

"Tastes great," said Mike. "Guys, I just wanted to say thanks for putting this together. It's been awesome to get on the gas with you, even if I did have to watch Rick spin around a pole in his underwear. TJ, I know this was all your idea. Thanks for being a great team leader and an even better friend."

The others raised their beers in agreement and they sat in the sun, enjoying the meal.

Ten minutes later TJ tossed his empty into the cooler. "OK, let's get back on the damn river before Rick starts bitching again. We've got the afternoon to cover twenty miles of class five rapids. This is the bit that separates the men from the pole dancers."

Chapter Eight

Revitalized by breakfast and a morning at the day spa Ali stepped out of the minivan into a picturesque park. Lush green grass met the waters of a wide slow-moving river lined with majestic swaying trees.

"This is magical," said Ali as the other girls joined her.

A loud bark sounded and she spotted Axe running toward them with a bright red ribbon around his neck. The dog made a beeline for her, barking excitedly. She dropped to a knee and he licked her face. "Hey buddy, you smell good. Have you had a bath?"

Leonie gave him a pat. "Maria organized a groomer. He spent the morning getting pampered. OK Axe, are you going to show us the way?"

The dog let out a bark and trotted off through the park toward a thick grove of trees. The girls followed.

"Is this where we're meeting Mike and the boys?" asked Ali as they followed a path into the woods.

"Yeah, in a few hours. There's fun to be had before then."

A row of ribbon tied trees lined the path as they approached a clearing. Ali let out a squeal of delight as she spotted a table laden with cakes and teapots. Around it strewn on the grass were croquet mallets, a ring toss, lawn balls and other games. A smaller table adorned with long-stemmed glasses stood next to a steel tub filled with champagne bottles.

In among the fairytale setting stood Maria in a beautiful summer dress. "Ladies, welcome to the bachelorette's delights."

She pressed a remote control and music filled the garden setting.

"Maria, this is beautiful," gushed Ali as she wrapped her arms around the buxom Latino.

"We couldn't have Leonie running the whole event. Like I said last night, someone had to bring a touch of class."

The other women gathered around the table.

Leonie pointed to a tree of cupcakes. "Oh look, little cock cakes."

Ali leaned closer and saw each of the hand-made cakes had an iced penis drawn on it.

"Wait till you see the lawn games," Maria said with a chuckle.

After the ladies enjoyed the afternoon snacks their host directed them to the equipment. "Ladies, high tea in the forest isn't complete without penis-themed games."

Ali started off with the ring toss, and threw an oversized plastic ring at the dildo serving as a peg. She missed. "Damn it."

Leonie stepped up for her go. "I really hope you're better at that with Mike."

"I generally don't throw anything this large at Mike's penis," replied Ali.

Leonie giggled and tossed, missing by yards. "It's harder than it looks."

Ali shook her head, laughing. "This has been a fantastic few days," she said as Maria joined them. "Thank you so much."

"My dear girl, it's our pleasure," said Maria.

Leonie nodded in agreement and then gestured to where Axe was enjoying a bone. "Even the hound is having a good time." She tossed another ring, missing again. "Screw this, I'm out." Dropping the rings, she downed her champagne.

Ali made a throw. "I wonder how the boys are doing?"

Leonie topped up her glass. "They'll be having a great time on the river." She checked her watch. "Only an hour till they arrive."

Ali tossed another ring. "I feel like we should organize some food for them."

Leonie raised her glass. "Already done. Maria has chow and coffee ready to go."

She tossed another ring. This time it fell directly on the rubber dildo. She jumped up and down in excitement. "I did it. I landed one."

Rick strained to hear TJ's orders over the roar of the hundreds of thousands of gallons of water smashing over and around massive granite boulders. The little raft bucked and twisted as they maneuvered it with deft strokes.

Then as suddenly as the wild section of the river started, it ended and they found themselves in calm water.

"Damn, that's hectic," yelled Rick as he leaned back against the raft and held his paddle across his knees.

"That was a grade four," said TJ. "There's two sets of grade five-plus in the next stretch. If you guys don't move a little faster when I give commands we'll end up in the drink."

"Keep your pants on, old man," said Rick. "We've been handling it like pros. Plus it's not like we can't swim, we're SEALs."

"The Meat Grinder doesn't give a crap what you are. You go in and you're in serious trouble."

"The Meat Grinder?" Dean sounded a little uncertain.

Rick laughed. "He's just trying to scare you."

"We'll see."

They cruised with the flow of the river for a few minutes before the familiar roar of rapids could be heard.

Rick readied himself for the onslaught. The roaring increasing in intensity as they approached a bend.

"Right side forward!" bellowed TJ.

He dug his paddle and the raft made its way to the outside of the bend narrowly avoiding a large rock. As they rounded the corner the rest of the rapids came into view. "Oh shit," murmured Rick as he surveyed the raging torrent of white water forcing its way between two huge boulders.

"Forward!" yelled TJ.

Together they paddled as the Chief aimed them for the gap.

Through the torrent Rick could see a crest of water then more boulders and rapids. He felt the raft gain speed as it was sucked into the chute. Water lashed his face and the craft bucked wildly as they entered the maelstrom.

"Right back!" screamed TJ over the noise.

Rick paddled hard spinning the raft. They dropped over

a small waterfall into a whirlpool where they surfed for a moment before TJ angled them clear.

"Left back."

He paddled frantically before realizing he'd messed up. They bounced off a massive boulder and slipped down a crevasse slightly narrower than the boat. It wedged firm and tons of water tipped them downward. TJ disappeared under the raft and then it broke free, flipping end over end.

Caught beneath it Rick managed to keep his legs up as the raft bounced through the rapids. Then suddenly it was gone and he was jetting through the rapids alone. He fought to keep his head above water as he was pumped through another set of small waterfalls. A boulder dealt him a solid blow, robbing him of feeling in his right arm.

The pummeling felt like it went on for minutes, but in reality it was a matter of seconds before he was clear of the rapids.

"Rick!"

He turned toward the voice and spotted Mike towing Dean toward the bank. Striking out with his good arm he kicked toward them. Behind him, another voice called out.

"Where's TJ?" Ernie caught up with him. "I can't see the raft or TJ."

The two men reached the shore together where Mike was supporting a coughing Dean. "Everyone OK?" he asked.

Rick wriggled his fingers. The feeling was slowly returning to his hand. "I'm good."

Dean coughed the last of the water from his lungs and gave thumbs up.

"TJ is gone." Ernie scanned the river with a concerned expression.

"He was first in. So he's probably further downstream. Don't worry, the old man knows the river," said Rick.

Once they were all out of the water Mike led them along the river, scrambling over boulders in search of TJ. As they hunted Rick spotted something blue ahead. They got closer and he saw it was their cooler. The Chief was sitting on the bank next to it. The raft was nowhere to be seen.

Rick crouched next to him. "TJ, you alright?"

"I would be if you listened to instructions," growled the veteran SEAL. "Caught my ankle under a rock." He gestured to his naked foot. The ankle looked red and swollen. "Lost my bootie and twisted it pretty bad."

"Thought we'd lost you," said Ernie.

"In this pissy river?" scoffed TJ.

"But, the meat grinder," added Dean.

The Chief laughed. "I made that up. It's actually called The Chute. Level four plus." He turned to Rick. "I don't suppose you've got a med kit, Corpsman?"

Rick shrugged off the backpack he wore over his life vest. Inside were his water bladder and a small medical kit. He never went anywhere without one.

"So what now?" asked Mike as Rick strapped TJ's ankle.

"Well, without a raft we've only got one option. We walk out."

"Follow the river downstream?" asked Ernie.

TJ shook his head. "No, the terrain gets worse. It would take us all night." He pointed up the bank. "We head due west till we hit one of the fire trails."

"Why don't we call for help?" asked Dean as he fished a plastic bag out of his life vest. Inside was his cell phone.

"No coverage up here, son." TJ selected a branch from a pile left by the river. He snapped off the end and used it to help him climb the riverbank. "We get going and we might be out of here by nightfall."

"Leonie, do you think something has happened to them?" Ali sat with a blanket wrapped around her shoulders on the bank of the river. "I mean, they were supposed to be here two hours ago, right?"

The girls had finished their high tea and moved to the agreed meeting point to receive the boys. Maria had organized their food on picnic tables in anticipation of hungry mouths.

"Something might be holding them up," said Maria. "You know TJ, he always plans for everything. They'll be along soon."

Ali turned to where Axe was sitting watching the river. The dog seemed to have a sixth sense when it came to locating Mike. His tongue lolled from his mouth and he wore an unconcerned expression. "Yeah, I'm sure everything is OK."

As they waited, the girls recounted the antics of the last twenty-four hours. Before long they were all giggling as they drank champagne left over from the high tea.

Another fifteen minutes passed without their arrival. Ali turned when she heard the sound of a car pulling into the parking lot. Her heart skipping a beat when she saw it was a park ranger's truck.

A tall female ranger walked across the lawn toward them. "Hi guys, I take it the rafters haven't arrived yet?"

Ali rose to greet her. "You don't have any news?"

The woman shook her head. "No, I met the boys last

night when I ran a class for them. TJ told me they'd be arriving around now."

"You ran a class for them?" asked Ali.

"Sorry." She held out her hand. "My name's Jenny. I run a pole dancing fitness class in town as well as being a park ranger."

Ali took her hand and introduced the other women.

"I'm confused, pole dancing?" said Leonie.

She laughed. "Yeah, I think Rick was a little confused too. He thought he'd hired a stripper, not a pole dancing instructor."

"Tell me you made them try it."

Jenny flashed a cheeky smile. "Of course I did. Rick decided he had something to prove."

"I hope someone got it on camera," said Ali.

"What happens at pole camp stays at pole camp." She took out her phone and showed them a picture of Rick inverted.

"Do you think they're all right?" asked Ali when the laughter had subsided.

"There's any number of reasons they might have been delayed."

"But, they're now two hours late."

"I'll radio into headquarters and find out if anyone has seen them. The river usually has a little traffic this time of year."

"Thanks, that would be great."

"In the meantime, you should sit tight. I'm sure the boys will be along shortly."

Chapter Nine

"TJ, that ankle's not looking good," Rick said as they rested. He had removed his life vest and rolled his wetsuit down to his hips. His helmet now hung from his backpack. They'd been on the move for an hour, but had made little progress.

The Chief sat on the ground opposite his wetsuit unzipped and swollen ankle raised on a log.

Dean, Mike and Ernie had also ditched their safety gear and were in various states of undress.

Rick passed his water bladder to TJ. Sweat was streaming down the Chief's face, his features contorted with pain.

"We should think about sending guys ahead to get comms and organize an evac. Because at this rate, we're not going to be back in time for the wedding."

TJ grabbed his stick and used it to stand. "I can walk."

"Sure you can, Gandalf. Guys, this isn't workable. I propose you head up to the spur and find the track. I'll stay with the Chief and we'll make our way up slow time."

Mike shook his head. "We should stay together."

TJ took a tentative step and grunted. "No. For the first time ever, Rick's right. I'm not going to be able to walk out anytime soon."

"You sure?" asked Ernie.

"Yeah, look it's easy to find the track. Keep heading uphill. Then turn right and follow it down till it hits a road. You should be able to get a call out there or flag someone down. You need to contact Leonie or Ali." He glanced at his watch. "We've missed our RV by three hours. They're going to be a little concerned."

Mike nodded. "Yeah, Ali is going to be stressed if we don't make contact soon. OK boys, let's move fast."

They left Rick and TJ sitting in the shade of a tree and began climbing the steep slope toward the ridgeline. The going was tough, hampered by thick vines and shrubs. Mike led the way, pushing a path through the undergrowth. They'd managed half a mile when he halted for a break.

As they sat, Ernie clawed at the crotch of his wetsuit. "Is anyone else getting chafed?"

"Like a bastard," said Dean as he fanned his face with his hand. He peered through some bushes and frowned. "Hey, what's that? Looks like some kind of netting."

Mike scanned the undergrowth. He didn't see anything until the wind picked up and he spotted what looked like a camouflage net, flapping in the breeze.

"Might be a camp," said Dean. "We should check it out." He pushed into the bushes with Mike and Ernie close behind.

The vegetation suddenly thinned and they found themselves standing in a plantation of tall bright green plants.

Mike looked up and saw that there were camouflage nets strung high in the trees.

"Wow! That's a lot of weed," said Dean.

Mike turned to Ernie who wore a concerned expression. "We need to get the hell out of here."

"It's a little late for that."

The voice came from behind them. They turned and found themselves staring into the barrel of a pump-action shotgun. The man that held it wore a denim shirt, dirty jeans and a ten-gallon hat. A fierce scowl adorned his face. "What the hell are you doing in our fields?"

"Look, our raft capsized on the river. We're hiking out to the track so we can get home."

The corner of the man's mouth lifted in a snarl. "Bullshit."

"Hey, essé we don't usually go hiking in wetsuits," snapped Ernie.

His eyes narrowed. "You better come with me." He used the barrel of the shotgun to direct them through the plantation.

Mike caught Ernie's eye and the Latino clenched his fist. He shook his head. There were too many variables. They didn't know if there were other men in the plantation. "Hey bud, we're not looking for trouble. We just need to find our way out of the woods so I can get to my wedding next week."

"Yeah, well you'll have to ask Travis."

"Who's Travis?" said Mike as they walked through the marijuana crop.

"You'll find out soon enough."

The plantation was sizeable. Nothing like the scale of the operations Mike had seen in Afghanistan, but still at least a dozen acres of plants hidden under camouflage netting.

A minute later they arrived at what he guessed was the caretaker's cabin. It was smaller than TJ's, run down with a sloping verandah that looked on the verge of collapsing. To one side was a large steel cage with a doghouse inside. He glanced around but couldn't see any dogs.

"Hold it there," said their captor. "Travis!" he bellowed.

A thumping sound emanated from the cabin and the door swung open revealing a morbidly obese man wearing coveralls. "Who the fuck are these guys?"

"I found them in the crop."

Travis scrutinized them through squinted eyes. "They look like cops."

Mike shook his head. "We're not cops, we're rafters who capsized on the river. If you'd point us in the direction of the closest road, we'll get out of your hair."

The fat man's forehead creased as he frowned and pulled a pistol from under his singlet. "Put them in the cage. Carter will know what to do with them."

"What? Are you kidding me?" Mike took a step forward. "You can't lock people up–" He felt a sharp pain in the back of his head, and his legs buckled. The last thing he remembered before he blacked out was hitting the ground face first.

The light was fading fast as Jenny pulled her pickup into the parking lot of the ranger station. Ali rode alongside her. "Is the Malinois yours?" she asked as they left the vehicle and walked into the building.

"He's Mike's, my fiancé."

Jenny held the door open for her. "He's a beautiful dog. I used to have Shepherds when I was a girl."

Ali's phone beeped as they walked through the foyer of the log-walled station into the operations room. A single ranger sat behind a bank of computer screens with his feet on the desk.

The message was an update from Maria who was still at the park. The other girls had returned to the resort with Leonie.

"Jenny, that was Maria. The guys still haven't arrived."

"OK." The ranger turned to her colleague. "Ben have we had any news?"

He lowered his feet and checked a screen. "No, nothing since this morning. Some guy called TJ rang in at 0930 to log his rafting trip. Nothing heard since."

"OK, I think it might be time to contact the Sheriff's Department." She reached for a phone and hit a speed dial button.

Ali waited as Jenny spoke to someone on the line passing on the details of the rafting expedition. She tried to reassure herself that Mike and the others were safe. Something may have happened, but Mike and the team were highly trained professionals. What's more, Rick was an experienced medic. None of it stopped her from worrying.

Jenny wore a glum expression as she returned the phone to its cradle. "Sheriff's department won't take any action until they've been missing for at least 48 hours."

"48 hours!"

"Yes, they're hamstrung by policy. Look, we can't do a lot tonight. Tomorrow I can organize a helicopter to give the river a once over. That's if they don't turn up before then."

"You sure there's nothing we can do?"

Jenny placed a hand on her shoulder. "The terrain in there is too rough for vehicles. We'd have to hike in and we can't do that when it's dark."

Ali considered her options. "Can we go at first light?"

"Hike in?"

"Yes, surely there's a spot where we can start looking."

Jenny walked across to a map pinned to the wall. "We could hike in to Granite Hut and then down to the five-mile rapids. If they've gotten in trouble, that's where they'll be."

"Then that's where we need to go. I'll bring Axe, he can find Mike anywhere."

"OK, if they don't turn up by dawn we'll hike in and locate them." She ran a critical eye over Ali's summer dress and flats. "You got any outdoor gear?"

"Yes, I came prepared to hike."

"Good, I've got everything else we'll need. I'll drop you back at the resort. Ben will call if he gets anything."

Ali scribbled her number on a slip of paper. "Thank you so much Jenny, you too Ben."

"It's all part of the job. I'm sure we'll find the boys safe and sound tomorrow."

Rick pulled his wetsuit back on and sat with his back against a tree, shivering. "Surely they would have made it out by now."

TJ was sitting a few feet away trying to light a fire using the battery from his cell phone and a chewing gum wrapper. "They'll have only just reached the road. It might take some time for them to organize a recovery team. I think we're going to be spending the night here."

"What! TJ, I'm starving." He watched as the Chief fiddled with the phone. A glow emitted from his hands and a second later he had a flame. It quickly took to a small ball of dried moss, gaining intensity. TJ fed it branches as it increased in size. Happy it was established he grabbed an energy bar from his pack and tossed it to Rick.

"Thanks, brother." He snapped off half and made to toss it back.

TJ waved him off as he fed logs into the fire. "I've got a few more."

"OK, so what do we do now?" he asked between mouthfuls.

The Chief inspected a piece of wood carefully and tossed it into the darkness. "Well, you need to find some dry wood, so we don't freeze to death."

He finished the bar and climbed to his feet. "That I can do."

"Don't go too far, it's easy to get lost out here."

"Yes Gandalf, I won't wander too far into Mirkwood."

"What the hell are you talking about?"

"Lord of the Rings."

"The movie?"

"No, the books." Rick shook his head. "Never mind. OK, I'll head uphill. At least then I know down is the way back."

"Good plan. You're full of surprises tonight."

Rick laughed. "Because I know how to avoid getting lost?"

"No, I didn't think you could read. Now go get some wood before this fire burns out."

Rick grinned. "Asshole."

He pushed his way through the bushes then waited for his eyes to adjust before searching for dry wood. With so many trees it shouldn't be that hard. He found a large dead log and started pulling pieces from it. The rotten wood came away in his hand. It was damp and moldy.

Walking another twenty yards up the hill he remembered back to the survival course he'd attended in fleet. One of the instructors had mentioned something about dry bark on the leeward side of trees.

He picked a large elm and searched around the trunk. Sure enough one side of it was completely dry. It took him a few minutes to collect an armful of the thick bark. Then he made his way back to their makeshift camp.

As he got closer he heard voices. He stopped and listened; someone was talking to the Chief. Voices carried in the cold night air. It was two men and they sounded angry.

He lowered the bark and crept forward until he could see the figures in the glow of TJ's fire.

"Are you alone?" snapped a deep voice.

"My friends went for help. They should be back soon."

If TJ was lying about Rick being nearby, there was a damn good reason for it. TJ had identified the men as a potential threat.

"What happened to your foot?" asked the voice again.

"I already told you. Our raft flipped and I got caught in the rapids. Look, I don't know what your problem is, but where I'm from you offer an injured stranger help. Not threats."

"There's no help coming for you. We've already got your buddies," said another in a nasal voice.

"Shut up," the deep voice ordered.

Rick's heart sank as he realized Mike and the others had been captured. He caught a glimpse of a shotgun in one of the men's hands.

The deep voice barked again. "Get on your feet. You're coming with us."

"I can't walk."

"It wasn't a goddamn question."

Rick crouched in the darkness with his fists clenched,

watching as one of the men hauled the Chief to his feet. The other stood with his weapon held ready.

The way he saw it he had two options. One, he could attack the men and risk them killing TJ, or two, he could follow from a distance and look for an opportunity to free the Chief and the others. He opted for the latter.

Rick tailed TJ and his captors from a distance. Thankfully the woods were damp and he was able to move silently through the bushes and vines.

They pushed the Chief into a thick grove of plants. It wasn't till he was among them that the pungent smell of marijuana filled his nostrils. "Holy shit, pot growing rednecks," he whispered.

He crept through the field, following the voices of the men as they yelled for the injured SEAL to move faster. Soon he saw lights from a dwelling.

Lowering to his stomach he crawled forward till he spotted a low-slung cabin. There was a large metal cage to one side of it and in the glow of the single bulb under the verandah he spotted Ernie, Dean and Mike. They were locked inside. "Fuck."

The two men directed the Chief to sit on the cabin's deck. Then the front door opened and a horrendously over-weight man waddled out. He reminded Rick of a redneck version of the *Star Wars* character, Jabba the Hutt.

"What the hell, another cop?" the man bellowed. "Carter is going to lose his shit."

Rick made a mental note of the name.

"Put him in the cage with the others."

He watched as they manhandled TJ into the cage and locked it with a thick chain.

"You keep watch. I'm going to call Carter." Jabba waddled back inside.

Rick now knew there was a phone in the cabin. He just needed to come up with a plan to lure the yokels away, immobilize Jabba, and free the guys. Not too hard a job for a SEAL.

"Hey, you guys better let us go!" The voice was Dean's. He stood, gripping the bars. "These guys are Navy SEALs and there's still another one out there."

"Dean, shut the hell up," mouthed Rick as Mike grabbed his brother and silenced him.

The taller of the two, with the deep voice, strode across to the makeshift prison and aimed his shotgun at them. "I don't give a fuck who you are, shut the hell up."

The second man bashed on the door of the cabin. "Travis, there's another one out there."

Jabba reappeared and stared out into the plantation with beady eyes. "Carter's sending up the boys. If there's another one we'll find him."

Rick's heart skipped a beat. He needed to get the hell out of the park and find help ASAP. He wiggled backward into the plantation. First things first he had to orientate himself and locate the track out of the park. Pushing out of the dope farm into a clearing he searched the sky. Finding the big dipper he traced a line through the top two stars to the North Star. Now at least he knew which way to go.

Chapter Ten

Rick pushed through thick vines cursing under his breath as he extracted himself from their clutches and checked his watch. He'd been moving uphill for the better part of five hours. Sitting in a clearing he wiped the sweat from his brow. Surely he should have hit the fire trail by now. In the starlight he noticed that the clearing extended away from him to the west. A turn of his head confirmed it did the same in the opposite direction. Finally, he'd found TJ's damn track.

He rested for a moment longer and then started off along the overgrown trail. Without the thick undergrowth he was able to break into a slow jog. The chafing from his wetsuit restricted his movement to more of a fast hobble.

As he jogged he ran through his plan in his head. He would get to town, alert the local authorities, and of course Ali, and then contact his boss, Commander Conner. The SEAL officer had contacts in the DEA. They would sort these pot-growing hicks out in no time.

Fixated on justice he almost missed the distant snarl of a

small engine. There was a flash of lights and Rick leaped off the track into the bushes. Seconds later the first of two buggies roared past. In the headlights of the second vehicle he spotted a bloodhound sitting in the bed of the ATV. Other buggies raced past with more men, some wielding firearms. Jabba had assembled a posse of hunters.

Rick now faced a major dilemma. If he stuck to the track the dogs would be able to easily sniff him out and the buggies run him down. As much as he hated the thought he needed to use the cover of the woods.

A glance at the sky identified the North Star and orientated him. Then he shoved his way into the bushes and started walking. Behind him he heard the buggies roaring into the distance.

Mike and the others sat huddled together in the filthy cage in an attempt to keep warm. The rubber of their wetsuits gave them a little insulation, but not enough to ward off the temperature drop that came with early dawn.

All four men turned when the sound of engines reached them. They watched as two ATVs arrived at the front of the cabin. Gun-toting hicks climbed from the vehicles and reported to Travis, the obese caretaker. A dog gave a long howl from the back of one of the buggies.

"I'm sorry guys," managed Dean between chattering teeth. "I should have kept my mouth shut."

TJ grasped his shoulder. "Not your fault, bud."

They listened as Travis addressed his posse of four gunmen. "Good thing y'all got here quick. Because we got ourselves a major problem." He gestured to cage. "These assholes stumbled on the crop. They've got government written all over them. There's one more out there trying to get out of the park." He held up a life vest. "Carter wants him alive." Tossing the flotation device to the men he waddled back inside the cabin.

One of the men released the bloodhound from the Polaris. It jumped down and sniffed the vest.

"Oh shit," murmured Mike.

The dog let out a howl and dashed toward the cage. It sniffed the air, circled and then darted into the drug plantation. A moment later it let out a blood-curdling bay.

"What the hell does that mean?" asked Dean.

"It means he's got Rick's scent," Mike whispered.

"He'll get away, though, right?" asked Dean.

"Damn straight he will," said TJ.

"He's a SEAL essé," he'll run rings around these yokels," added Ernie.

In the gloom, Mike caught the grim look on TJ's face. They needed to come up with an escape plan.

Ali gripped the Ford pickup's grab handle as it lurched over rocks and struggled for grip. Behind the wheel Jenny activated the diff lock and eased the truck forward. Spotlights illuminated the track in front of them, revealing a heavily rutted trail.

"Your sister and Maria are great," said Jenny as they bounced over another boulder.

"Yeah, they're the best."

Jenny had picked her up at the resort at a little past four in the morning. Leonie and Maria had already been up packing sandwiches and coffee. They'd dropped the two women at the ranger station where they had insisted on helping man the phones in the operations room. The women knew they would be a liability in the field but that didn't stop them from helping.

The truck rocked sideways and there was a bark from the rear of the dual cab.

"I don't think Axe likes my driving."

"Yeah, well I do. The further we go in the truck the less we have to walk, right?"

"Exactly." Jenny changed gears as the track smoothed.

"I know I've said this a dozen times, but thank you."

Jenny turned and smiled at her. "Hey, it's nothing. I love getting out in the park. Your guys looked capable. I'm sure they've camped up for the night. We'll find them in no time."

Ali nodded. "Yeah." She sat silently as they wound their way up a hill. Minutes passed before a wide clearing appeared in the spotlights.

Jenny brought the truck to a halt and killed the engine. "This is far as we can drive."

They climbed out of the cab and Ali snapped a lead onto Axe's collar. Jenny handed her a backpack before reaching for her own.

"Base this is Jenny, over," the ranger spoke into her radio.

A moment later Maria's voice replied. "Go ahead, Jenny."

Jenny smiled. "Wow, already on the airwaves." Lifting the radio to her mouth, she replied, "Base, we've reached Whistler's clearing. My handheld will probably drop out soon. We'll check in at Granite Hut no later than zero nine hundred."

"No problems," replied Maria. "The chopper will be flying through at zero six thirty."

"Copy that, Jenny out." She adjusted a headlamp then took a pump action shotgun from the truck and strapped it to the side of her bag. "Right, let's get moving."

Ali activated her own light and gripped Axe's lead tight as she followed the ranger along a track into the woods. The dog stepped out in front, pulling eagerly.

They only needed their lamps for another half hour. Soon the soft glow of dawn penetrated the forest and it came alive with the call of birds.

"It's so beautiful," said Ali as they descended a steep ravine.

"Beats the hell out of working in an office."

"You said you were a lawyer, right?"

"Worked corporate law in New York for almost ten years. Came out here to escape."

"And is there a Mr. Park Ranger?"

She shook her head. "No. I had a guy in New York. He turned out to be a thief and a cheat."

"Oh, so sorry to hear that."

"My fault for dating a banker."

They reached the bottom of the gully and Jenny unslung her backpack. "How about we have a short break? Coffee and a sandwich?"

"Sounds good." Ali's stomach had been grumbling for the last fifteen minutes.

Jenny poured coffee from a flask as Ali unwrapped the sandwiches. Axe licked his chops as he sat at her feet.

"So, was Axe a military dog?" asked Jenny as she sipped.

"Still is, he and Mike are teammates."

Jenny reached over and ruffled his ears. "He's a handsome boy."

As they ate Ali heard a faint sound in the distance. The noise grew louder and she identified it as a helicopter.

Jenny unhooked her radio. "That'll be the search chopper." She checked the channel guide taped to the back and made an adjustment. "Fire Spotter, this is Jen."

Ali looked up through the forest canopy for the helicopter as she listened.

"Jenny, this is Ed. You down there?"

"Yeah, we're on our way to Granite Hut."

"Roger, look we spotted what we think is a raft on Whistler's Bend. No sign of any bodies though."

Ali's heart leaped as she locked eyes with Jenny.

"OK, Ed. Look, we're not far away. We'll go down and take a look."

"Roger, I'll do one more pass and then I'm heading back to base."

"Thanks, bud." Jenny reattached the radio to the shoulder strap of her backpack. "Ali, this is a good thing. If they got separated from their raft they'll be trying to walk out. No mean feat in this terrain. We'll head down to the bend and check it out. Any luck, we'll meet up with them on the way."

Rick skidded down a steep slope, snagged a branch on his wetsuit and lost his footing. Tumbling through the bushes he rolled off a ledge and hit the ground with an almighty thud. On his back he stared up through the forest canopy. "Fuck my life."

As he lay motionless a chopper thundered overhead. He jumped to his feet ignoring the chafing between his legs and ran in the direction of the aircraft. A moment later, realizing how futile the gesture was, he sat on a boulder and gathered himself.

Things had gone wrong when he was forced to abandon the track and make his own way through the thick forest. ATVs racing along the trail had pushed him further and further off course until he was well and truly lost. He knew he was somewhere between the river and the ridgeline.

Taking his phone from his backpack he powered it up; still no reception. His stomach growled loudly, reminding him that he hadn't eaten since the night before.

He sipped water from the bladder in his pack and slung it over his shoulder. Then as he was about to set off there was a rustle in the bushes.

Turning slowly he spotted a large black shape among the foliage. A bear emerged from the undergrowth and sat on its haunches. It inspected him through small inquisitive eyes.

Rick's pulse raced as his brain screamed orders to his legs to turn and run. "Jenny said you were more afraid of me than I am of you. In which case, you must be scared shitless," he mumbled, fighting the urge to bolt.

The bear ambled forward and sat a few yards from him. Yawning it scratched its belly. Rick's heart rate dropped as he studied the animal. Jenny was right it didn't seem to be a threat. He spotted a tag in its ear and recalled that she'd said they were after easy food.

"Hey, I'm sorry. I haven't got anything to eat. In fact, I'm starving. So if you could point me in the direction of a Jack in the Box that would be killer."

The animal turned its head away from him, angling its ears up the hill.

"What can you hear?"

Suddenly the bear rose and dashed past Rick, disappearing into the bushes. A moment later the baying of a dog reached his ears. "Oh shit." He turned and sprinted after the bear.

———

Mike inspected the lock on the heavy chain that secured the cage as he rubbed the lump on the back of his head.

"What's the prognosis?" asked TJ.

He sighed. "Nothing serious, just a bruise."

"No, the lock."

"Oh, not good. This is high-grade and the chain's tempered steel. We need to find another way out."

The sound of the cabin door opening caught his attention. He watched as a tall square-jawed cowboy appeared. He wore a Stetson, jeans, checked shirt and a pistol on a belt with an oversized buckle. At a guess, this was the boss, Carter.

The man swaggered across to the cage and stood in front of them with his thumbs tucked behind his buckle. "So, these are our nation's finest." He sniffed and spat in the dust. "Y'all gonna tell me what you were doing sniffing around my business?"

"Looking for Bin Laden?" replied TJ, deadpan.

"Hilarious. Didn't you guys already kill him?"

"That's what the government wants you to believe," added Ernie.

"Regular fucking comedians, aren't ya."

"We try," said TJ. "Now, how about you let us out before you find yourself in a whole lot of trouble that you don't need."

Carter flashed a broad smile. "Yes, sir. Right away. While I'm at it, I'll whip you up some eggs for breakfast."

He took a step closer. "You smart ass city boys better enjoy your last few hours. Because, as soon as I find your friend I'm gonna let the river finish what it started."

Behind him, Travis appeared carrying a water jug and a funnel with a length of hose attached to it. The overweight caretaker dumped the items alongside a chair.

"Y'all get some rest now." Carter turned and returned to the cabin.

"What the hell is that for?" Dean gestured to the funnel and hose.

"They're going to fill us full of water and dump us in the river," replied TJ. "That way, everyone will assume we drowned."

Mike rattled the bars in frustration. "Four SEALs drown in a river. Are they stupid? No one is going to believe that."

"Don't count on it. This river has killed far more experienced rafting crews."

He turned from the bars with his jaw clenched. "And you thought it would be a good idea to bring a team of first timers out on it, the week before my wedding."

"Relax, we had it well in hand."

"Apart from the whole losing the raft and ending up in a drug baron's prison thing."

"I think baron is a long bow to draw. He's more of a weed growing yokel. Compared to Barbosa, he's *los bajos fondos*," added Ernie.

"Barbosa, I'd forgotten about that piece of shit. Why is it that every time you guys interfere with my love life it ends up involving a criminal?"

"To be fair, this hasn't got anything to do with your love life. It was just an excuse to get away and bond," said TJ.

"Yeah, well it's working. You don't get a better bonding

experience than being locked in a POW cage on a dope farm."

Dean managed a chuckle. "True, I mean you couldn't plan this shit."

Mike turned to TJ. "Now would be an excellent time to tell us this is all a hoax."

The look on the veteran SEAL's face told him it wasn't. They were actually facing death and it looked as if their only hope was Rick; a man who hated the outdoors even more than he hated his ex-wife.

Chapter Eleven

Ali and Jenny found the raft lodged between rocks on a bend in the river. From high on the bank the deflated craft resembled a discarded garbage bag submerged in a puddle.

They climbed over boulders to get a closer look. Fixated on the boat Ali slipped on the slimy surface. She threw an arm out to brace herself, but missed and toppled into a shallow pool, drenching her bag and clothing.

"Ali, are you OK?"

She grimaced in pain, clutching her arm to her chest as Jenny helped her from the water. Axe bounded across and licked her face as she sat on the bank. "So stupid."

"Show me your arm."

Ali extended the injured limb toward the ranger who inspected it.

"Wiggle your fingers."

She complied.

"Now clench your fist."

Pain shot through her forearm, but there was no impingement to the movement.

"It's not broken. However, it's pretty badly bruised."

"I'm so sorry, Jenny. I'm not usually this clumsy."

The ranger looked at her with kind eyes. "Hey, it's not your fault. You've got a lot on your mind." She took a map from her pocket. "The good news is there's no sign of the boys. So, I think they're walking out. If TJ is half the woodsman he seems to be they would have pushed up this ridgeline and down the track." She used a twig to show the route. "That means they would have reached Granite Hut. It's not far from here. We'll head over, get you dry, take another look at that arm and radio HQ. You think you're going to be right to walk?"

Ali nodded. "Yeah, I might be clumsy, but I'm not soft."

"I didn't think so. OK, let's get a move on."

It took Ali, Jenny and Axe a little under an hour to reach Granite Hut. The eight-bunk outpost got its name from an outcrop that was visible from the porch. Popular with climbers and hikers it was the main access point to the east of the park.

Jenny unlatched the door and placed her backpack on the table inside. Soon she had a fire lit in the iron stove and a kettle heating. "I've got a dry sweater in my pack."

Ali sat on a stool with her arm held across her chest. "Thanks, any chance you have some pain killers?"

Jenny pulled clothing and a medical kit from her pack. "Of course. How's the arm feeling?"

"Starting to swell."

Jenny tipped pills into the cap of a bottle, poured a cup of water from the cabin sink and handed them to Ali. "This should help."

She took the medication before struggling out of her wet T-shirt and slipping Jenny's sweater over her head. As she warmed in front of the stove Axe explored the cabin, sniffing every corner.

"Mike hasn't been here," she concluded when he sat at her feet.

Jenny strode across to a large steel cabinet and unlocked it with a combination. Inside were a radio and shelves loaded with search and rescue supplies. She turned on the radio, adjusted the frequency and spoke into the handset. "Base, this is Jenny at Granite Hut."

There was a pause then a hiss of static and finally a reply. "Jenny, good to hear from you. How are things going?"

Ali didn't recognize the voice.

"We found the raft near Whistler's Bend. No sign of the guys."

"OK, the chopper spotted movement about three miles due west of your location. Had to return to base before he could check it out."

Jenny turned to Ali and nodded.

"I'll take a look. Ali's injured her arm so she'll be staying here at Granite."

She shook her head at the ranger.

"Anything serious?"

"No, but I think it would be a good idea to have someone here in case they make it this far. Plus, I can use her as a relay back to you guys."

"Good idea."

"OK, well I'm going to go check out that sighting. Ali will radio in on the hour."

"Good luck."

Jenny secured the handset as the kettle whistled. She

lifted it from the stove and took two mugs from a cupboard. "I think it's better if you stay here. I need you to operate the radio in case I have to get in contact with the station. I'll be back in a few hours."

Ali winced as she raised her arm to take the coffee. "You're right. I'm only going to slow you down. I'm sorry." She glanced down at Axe who wore a concerned expression. "Take, Axe. If Mike is out there he'll find him."

"You sure he will be OK without you?"

The dog walked across to the door and scratched at it.

"I guess so," Jenny said as she grabbed her backpack.

Ali followed her out onto the porch. "You two be careful and please, bring the boys home."

Jenny embraced her in a hug. "With Axe's nose there's no way we won't find them."

Ali watched the dog and the ranger walk across the clearing. Axe turned at the edge of the woods and stared at her before letting out a reassuring bark. Then he disappeared after Jenny. She stood for a moment, staring after them. Then she returned to the cabin to man the radio.

Rick leaped over a log landed heavily and rolled. Jumping back to his feet he wiped the sweat from his brow and paused to listen.

A few hundred yards away the dog bayed. Then for the first time, he heard voices. The hunters were getting closer.

He started off through the woods, wincing as a rock punched through what remained of his dive booties. The shredded rubber footwear barely clung to his feet. His legs ached, he'd run out of water and the inside of his thighs were chafed to the point where he could feel the sting of raw flesh against the rubber.

Despite all that he wasn't going to stop. The rest of the team depended on him. He needed to get to a phone and get help.

The baying of the hound turned to frantic barking. With each outburst he could hear it getting closer. The men's shouting was also louder, accompanied now by the sound of them crashing through the undergrowth.

A wise man had once said, 'Don't run you'll only die tired'. It was a motto that Rick embodied. He was all about lifting iron, fighting hard and kicking his enemy in the teeth. Skidding to a halt, he tore a branch from a tree to use as a club. He took deep breaths, slowing his racing heart rate. Whatever happened next he was going to go down swinging.

The dog was the first to appear. It charged out of the bushes and spotted him, baring its teeth. Rick waved his homemade cudgel at it. "You want a piece of me?"

Snarling it charged forward, snapping its jaws.

Rick swung and the dog jumped clear. He didn't want to hurt the animal, but he saw no other way to escape.

"Hold it right there, muscles." He glanced in the direction of the voice and found himself looking down the barrel of a pump action shotgun. The man holding it wore camouflage pants and a USMC T-shirt.

A second man appeared. This one carried a lever action rifle and was dressed in a denim shirt, jeans and cowboy boots.

"You're pretty fast for a gym junkie," said the guy with the shotgun. "Now lower the stick or I'm going to blow your head off."

Rick's jaw was clenched, his muscles taught and ready to

leap into action. However, he knew he could never cover the dozen yards that separated him and the gunmen. His only hope was to jump behind a tree and sprint for cover.

"I know you're thinking about running. You do that and old Bones here will run you down," said the cowboy.

At the mention of its name the dog let out a savage growl.

Rick lowered his cudgel and came up with a new plan. He'd let the men get close then disarm one of them, knock out the other, deal with the dog and escape. The odds weren't in his favor, but it was better than giving up.

Suddenly, there was a low snarl from the bushes. The noise sent a shiver racing up his spine. Bones dropped his tail then whimpered and cowered on the ground.

The shotgun swung in the direction of the commotion.

"What the fuck is that?" asked the other man. "Doesn't sound like no bear."

"RICK, DOWN!" a familiar female voice yelled.

As he dropped to the earth a shotgun boomed. He caught a glimpse of a brown shape as it streaked from the bushes.

The hound yelped wildly and the men bellowed in terror as Axe attacked. The SEAL dog went directly for the camouflaged gunman. Axe ripped the shotgun from his hands then latched onto his arm. The man in the cowboy hat fled after his dog.

"Axe, stop!" screamed the woman's voice.

Rick watched as the dog released the hunter. The man turned and fled, crashing through the foliage. The shotgun boomed again, blasting leaves above his head.

"Damn, am I glad to see you," said Rick to Axe as the Malinois set upon him with a slobbery tongue. He let the dog lick his face as he turned to identify the shooter.

Jenny, the pole-dancing ranger, stepped from the bushes dressed in cargo pants and a green uniform shirt. She looked like someone from the Wild West with a pistol on her hip and a shotgun in the crook of her arm. "You look a little worse for wear, sailor."

Rick climbed to his feet, grinning.

"You're a god damn angel," he croaked from a parched throat.

"Axe is your angel." She took a canteen from her backpack and passed it to him. "He led me straight to you."

She gave him a moment to drink then handed him granola bars. He devoured two in a matter of seconds.

"We need to get help," he managed as he chewed.

"Is someone injured? Where are the others?" she asked, reloading her shotgun. "And who the hell were those guys?"

He took another sip from the bottle and then recounted the past sixteen hours to her.

She shook her head in disbelief. "That's crazy. I can't believe they've got an entire plantation growing up there. We need to get back and let the police know."

"More like the DEA. Do you have a radio?"

She nodded and unhooked it from her shoulder strap. "Ali, this is Jenny do you read me?"

"Ali's up here?"

She nodded as she listened for a reply. When she heard nothing, she tried again. There was still no response. "There could be interference. Are you right to walk with me to the hut?"

"Can we contact the authorities from there?"

"Yes, Ali's manning the radio back to my station."

"Excellent, let's get a move on then." He climbed to his feet and took a few tentative steps.

"Are you, OK?" she asked.

Rick screwed up his face. "Not really."

"Your feet?"

He shook his head. "My groin. The wetsuit has rubbed me raw."

She rummaged in her pack and produced a jar of Vaseline. "This works for me."

"You're an angel. This is literally the third time you've saved me."

She winked. "The bear doesn't count. Now hurry up and get lathered up so we can get out of here before those assholes come back." She strode across and recovered the shotgun the gunman had dropped. When she turned back he was screwing the lid on the jar. She waved it away when he offered it to her. "You keep it." Then she handed him the other gun. "Just in case we run into them again."

He checked the breech of the weapon. "I'm counting on that."

Chapter Twelve

Carter grabbed a half bottle of bourbon from a rickety table and tossed it against the wall. It smashed, dribbling the liquor down the grimy wood.

"How did you mess this up?" he screamed into his radio. "How did you let an unarmed wetsuit-wearing tourist get the drop on you?"

There was a hiss of static and then a sheepish reply. "He had help."

"From who? Yogi the damn bear?"

"No, a park ranger."

Carter turned and stared at Travis who was sitting wedged in a tatty recliner. "Just one?"

"Yeah, tall chick with a crazy dog. Came out shooting and the dog tore Carl up pretty bad."

He scowled at Travis. "I only know one tall female ranger, Jenny." He spoke into the radio. "Where are you now?"

"Back with our ATVs up on the ridgeline. I've bandaged up Carl's arm."

The deputy sheriff stormed across to the wall where a map of the park was nailed. He traced his finger from the ridgeline down to the main road out of the park. A few miles from Carl and Hank's location pointed at a small square, Granite Hut. He knew from experience that it was the only place you could get radio reception out to the ranger station. "They're heading to Granite," he spoke into his handset. "You need to get there first and stop them from getting a call out."

"What do you want us to do with them?"

"Whatever you have to, just bury the bitch deep."

"I was hoping you'd say that."

He tossed the radio on the table.

"We should kill those fucking SEALs," Travis said with a snort. "They're working for the man."

Carter's eyes narrowed. "Don't start that conspiracy crap with me. Until we have the other one we keep them alive. We get in a situation and they're the only bargaining chip we have."

"They're a liability, Carter. They've seen too much."

He glared at the fat man. "You're a god damn liability, Travis. If you had've taken care of this in the first place, I wouldn't be here cleaning up your mess."

"That's not fair."

Carter made for the door. "Life's not fair." He stepped out into the bright sunshine and squinted, donning his sunglasses. He turned and checked on his caged captives.

"Things not going your way?" asked the old guy with the busted ankle. "You know, if you let us out and show us to safety we'll forget any of this happened. You can be the hero that saved some lost rafters."

Carter eyeballed the man. "That's not how things work up here."

Jenny was impressed. Despite his injuries and lack of sleep and food Rick was moving fast. He was right on her heels as she jogged through the woods in the direction of Granite Hut. Axe, keen to return to Ali was scouting out in front.

As she jogged she found herself comparing the handsome SEAL to her ex in New York. Sam, a cocksure banker had been utterly full of himself. He'd continually boast about making mulit-million dollar deals and holding people's jobs in his hand. Yes, he was handsome and yes, the sex was fantastic, but in the end it couldn't make up for his utter lack of humility and empathy.

Rick on the other hand was a man who had reasons to be proud. He was an elite operative and a decorated veteran. Yet, there was vulnerability about him. He might be a bit of a show boater, but he didn't take himself too seriously. He'd proven that with his attempt at pole dancing. He also had an undying loyalty to his friends and loved ones. Of course it also helped that he was about as chiseled and handsome as a man could get.

"Jenny, you hear that?"

Rick's voice snapped her back to their current situation. She paused and over her breath she heard the snarl of ATVs. "They're heading for the cabin."

She broke into a run. Ahead, Axe disappeared into the undergrowth. The dog seemed to sense that Ali was in danger.

Suddenly, Rick dashed past her with the shotgun held ready. He plowed through the undergrowth like a bulldozer. She tried to match his speed, but fell behind.

The noise of the buggies grew louder and then started to fade as they pulled ahead. Jenny guessed they would reach Granite Hut in a matter of minutes. Meanwhile, she and Rick were at least fifteen away. She slowed and talked into her radio. "Ali, this is Jenny. Do you read me?"

There was a burst of static.

"Ali, this is Jenny, if you can hear me you need to get out of the hut. I say again, you need to get out of the hut."

Ali abandoned her attempt to reply to Jenny over the radio, stuffed her things in her backpack and slung it over her shoulder as she made for the door.

She'd heard rather than saw the buggies that arrived outside. Frantically searching the cabin for a hiding place she dropped her bag and slid in under one of the bunks. Pressing herself against the wall she fought to control her panic.

The door creaked as it opened. From her hiding place she could see two pairs of boots as they clumped inside. Cowboy boots and a pair of battered combat boots. The cowboy wore jeans with frayed cuffs. His partner wore camouflaged cargos not unlike those Mike wore to work.

The men moved around the cabin, searching.

"There's no one here," drawled a gruff voice.

The cowboy poked her backpack with the toe of his boot. "There was."

Her heartbeat sounded like a brass drum as she fought to keep her breathing low and shallow.

The combat boots strode across to the radio cabinet. "The handset's still warm."

Panic overwhelmed her and she pushed harder against the wall, willing it to open and swallow her.

"You going to come out from under there?" drawled the

cowboy as he stood in front of the bunk. "We ain't gonna hurt you."

"Yeah, we just want to talk to your friends."

"Shut the fuck up, Carl. Look, don't be scared. My friend's a bit stupid, but he's harmless."

Both pairs of boots were now standing a few feet from the bunk and pointing directly at her. Her only option was to crawl out and make a run for the door. "If you step back I'll come out."

There was a pause. She pictured the two men looking at each other, questioningly.

"OK."

The boots took a step back. She took a deep breath then crawled out from under the bed.

The men looked exactly how she pictured them. Cowboy wore a denim shirt and held a rifle. Camo Guy had a pistol clutched in one hand. The other was heavily-bandaged.

"What happened to you?" she asked in a soft voice.

"Bear," the man grunted.

Cowboy silenced him with a glare. "We're the ones asking the questions. Where's your ranger buddy?"

Ali feigned ignorance. "I don't know who you're talking about."

His eyes narrowed. "Don't fuck around with us, Missy."

She could tell by the look that he meant it.

"She left, I don't know when she'll be back."

"She's lying," said Camo Guy.

Cowboy spat on the floor. "Tie her hands. We'll take her back to Carter. He can decide what to do with her."

The pistol was thrust into her face and a moment later they spun her around, binding her wrists with tape. Camo

Guy shoved her through the door as Cowboy smashed the radio.

Outside two buggies were parked side by side. A morose looking Bloodhound sat on the back of one of them. Camo Guy gestured for her to climb into the passenger seat of the other. As she did the dog started whining.

"Bones, what the fuck's wrong with you?" said her captor as he climbed into the driver's seat.

There was a menacing growl from the opposite side of the buggy and the hound's whining intensified.

Ali recognized the sound instantly. She turned and saw Axe, hackles raised and teeth bared, standing a few yards away.

"Aw, shit." The man raised his pistol.

She shoved him with her shoulder and the gun went off, hitting the dirt.

Before he could recover Axe leaped onto the hood and pounced through the open roll cage, clamping his jaws on the man's bandaged arm. He screamed and the pistol was flung clear as the dog shook his arm, tearing flesh.

"Carl, get down!" yelled Cowboy from the porch. He had his rifle aimed at Axe.

Ali screamed. "No!"

The boom of a gun echoed off the mountains. A chunk blew out of the cabin wall next to Cowboy's head. As he ducked Ali turned and saw Rick storm out from the bushes. He had a shotgun held firm in his shoulder the barrel aimed unwaveringly at Cowboy. A tattered wetsuit covered his legs the top half hanging from his waist. He looked like he'd been through hell.

"Next one's on you," he bellowed.

Cowboy stood staring at the SEAL, his rifle held low.

Rick stopped ten yards short with the shotgun aimed directly at his chest. "I see that gun move and you're dead."

Axe had released the other man's arm and stood on the hood of the buggy, teeth bared and eyes fixed on his throat.

There was a rustle in the bushes and Jenny appeared with her gun raised. "Drop the rifle."

Outmatched, Cowboy let his weapon drop on the porch. "You people don't know who you're fucking with. Carter is going to be pissed."

"Carter? Lieutenant Carter Brown?" asked Jenny as she approached.

Cowboy realized he'd already said too much and buttoned his lips. Rick stepped onto the porch, kicked the rifle away, reversed his shotgun and drove the butt into the man's stomach."

He doubled over and dropped to his knees, groaning.

Rick bent down to whisper in his ear. "If anything's happened to my friends you're going to wish you never lived."

Jenny freed Ali and then found the roll of tape Carl had used to secure her. They bound both men's hands behind their backs and dumped them on a bunk with their feet taped.

"We can't get a call out," said Ali as she joined them with Axe by her side. "They smashed the radio."

Rick inspected the cabinet as Jenny poured him a mug of cold water from the sink. "Can you fix it?" she asked, handing the mug to him.

He prodded the shattered control panel with his finger. "Ernie could. I don't have the skills."

"We need to get a message out and alert the authorities," said Jenny.

Ali's gaze fell on the two buggies parked outside. "I could go."

Jenny shook her head. "No, we shouldn't split up again. We should all go."

"I'm not leaving without the others," said Rick in a low voice.

"You and Jenny can help free Mike and the others. I'll drive a buggy back to the main road and get help." She inspected one of them. "I had a Polaris on dad's farm. It'll be a piece of cake."

Rick nodded. "I think it's the best option."

Jenny frowned. "The forest is a maze of trails. You could get lost."

"This buggy's got a GPS. I can follow it straight out of the park."

Jenny considered the plan. "OK, let's do it."

"You girls sort that out," said Rick as he eyeballed the two men on the bunk. "I need to get out of this wetsuit."

Ali grabbed her backpack, carried it outside and tossed it in the buggy. She realized that the Bloodhound was missing. It must have run off into the woods.

The GPS was an expensive touch screen model with high-resolution maps. It took Jenny a matter of minutes to program a route for Ali.

As she finished Rick appeared from inside the cabin. He'd relieved Carl of his camouflage pants, hacked them off below the knee and somehow managed to squeeze into them. He'd also borrowed a USMC T-shirt that looked two sizes too small. With a pistol belt around his waist and a shotgun slung over his shoulder he looked like a cross between Rambo and a WWE wrestler.

"I'm going to start calling you Rickbo," said Jenny with a laugh as she climbed out of the buggy.

He managed a grin. "We need to get moving. We'll go on foot. They'll have the tracks leading to the plantation covered."

Ali started the buggy. "Axe should go with you. He'll find Mike and he's good in a fight."

Jenny nodded. "He's saved the day twice already."

"Just take care of him. I'll be back with help as soon as I can." She spun the buggy's wheels and took off into the woods.

Jenny turned to Rick who was rummaging through the other ATV. He stuffed a roll of tape, gas stove canisters and other items into his backpack along with boxes of cartridges for the pistol, shotgun and rifle he'd taken from the gunmen. He had one of the men's radios hooked to his belt.

"What's the plan?" she asked.

"Recon followed by direct action."

She watched him shrug the backpack over his broad shoulders and gather up the guns. The man oozed masculinity and confidence from every pore of his muscular body. Despite the seriousness of the situation she couldn't help but feel a little excited.

"What's up? Have I got something on my face?" he asked.

Realizing she was staring she blushed, turned away and started off up the hill. Axe fell in alongside her. "Come on, Rick. Let's get a hustle on."

Chapter Thirteen

Carter stood on the cabin's rickety porch with his radio held high in the air. Travis sat in a rocking chair next to him with a shotgun across his knees.

"That ain't going to help. Radio waves don't work that way."

"Oh, so you're an engineer all of a sudden. How about you shut your mouth and watch those prisoners."

Travis frowned and turned away from him.

"Yeah, sulk while I solve this damn problem." As he turned his attention back to the radio he spotted movement on the trail that led through the plantation. It was a dog. To be more precise it was Bones, Hank's dog. Something must have happened. That was why he wasn't getting a response on the radio.

"Fuck."

The dog made its way across to Travis and sat at his feet. "Carter, Bones wouldn't leave Hank."

"No shit." He changed the channel on the radio and called his deputies. "Ed, you read me?"

"Yeah, boss," came through immediately.

"I need you to get to Granite Hut. Is Harold with you?"

"Yeah, we found a truck down at Whistler's Clearing. It's one of the rangers."

"Goddamn Jenny," he said to himself. He depressed the transmit button. "Immobilize it and then get up to Granite. Something's happened to Carl and Hank."

"Yeah boss, you can count on us."

Carter stepped off the balcony and strode across to the cage where he locked eyes with the grizzled old SEAL, if that's what he actually was. "If your buddies killed any of my boys I'll slit your throat."

The man stared defiantly at him. Carter spat in the sand, turned and tossed his radio to Travis. "Watch them and keep an ear out." Then he disappeared inside.

A moment later the older guy called out from the cage. "Travis, I don't think he respects you very much."

The overweight yokel racked the action of his shotgun. "Shut the hell up."

"Just an observation. Looks like you do all the work around here and Carter gets to call the shots."

Travis pried himself from the chair and waddled across to the cage. "I know what you're trying to do G-man. Divide and conquer and all that stuff. I know exactly how you work, but it ain't gonna work on me."

"Hey, I'm just making an observation."

"Yeah, well keep them to yourself."

Ali slowed the buggy and came to a halt at a fork in the track. The GPS was struggling to keep up. She guessed it was because of the dense forest coverage. Idling she waited for the dash mounted device to update.

She didn't hear the two ATVs that appeared on the opposite track. The noise of her engine masked their approach. They blasted around the corner, nearly collided with her as they shot past. She watched in the mirror as they skidded to a halt in a cloud of dust.

The idea of asking them for help dissipated as quickly as she spotted a weapon in the mirror. One of the ATVs turned toward her. The other zoomed off in the direction of the hut.

Ali dropped her Polaris into gear and floored it. The thousand cc engine roared, wheels spun and she rocketed down the trail. Branches slapped the roll cage as she accelerated, her eyes watering as she hit forty miles an hour. A glance in the mirror confirmed that one of the buggies was in pursuit.

She gritted her teeth and pushed the throttle harder. People were depending on her. Mike depended on her.

Spotting a sandy section ahead she backed off the gas. Then as she entered a corner she put the Polaris into a controlled slide narrowly missing a tree as the road snaked back into the woods.

Gunshots rang out and bullets cracked past her head. One ricocheted off a roll bar punching a hole in the plastic roof.

Ali checked the mirror. Her pursuer was only a few yards behind, close enough for her to see it was one of Carter's deputies, Ed. "Son of a bitch." She braced and slammed on the brakes. The other buggy hit hers with a thud.

The driver wasn't prepared and was flung forward

against the steering wheel. Over her shoulder she saw a pistol fly through the air.

She rode the impact, accelerating away. The track was rocky and she tried to check the GPS as the buggy bounced down the ridgeline. A spinning icon told her it was useless.

The track took a hard left and dropped away. She wrenched the wheel and jumped on the brakes, wincing as it jerked her injured arm. Sitting high in the seat she peered over the hood. It was steeper than anything she'd attempted in her dad's farm buggy.

An engine roared behind her.

"Here goes nothing." She gripped the steering wheel tight and released the brake.

The little buggy gained speed as it slipped and skidded down what felt like a nearly vertical slope. Ali kept her foot clear of the brake, letting the gearbox manage the speed the best it could.

In the mirror she spotted the other ATV at the top of the slope. Ed handled the steep descent with skill. In a matter of seconds he was back on her tail.

The only saving grace was that he'd lost his weapon. Now he had to rely on his driving skills to stop her. What's more, from a glimpse of his machine she'd deduced it was an older Yamaha, inferior to the Polaris she'd borrowed. That didn't stop him from milking everything he could from the engine.

At the bottom of the descent the track dipped into a muddy stream. The wheels of Ali's buggy spun and she slid sideways off the path onto the opposite bank. The bushes were sparse so she ran with the alternate route. Snaking around rocks and logs she felt barely in control of the snarling vehicle. A glance over her shoulder confirmed that the Yamaha was still on her tail.

As the scrub thickened she was forced to slow. Her buggy roared shoving its way through the thick under-growth. Free to follow in her tracks the pursuer was soon right on her bumper.

"Pull over!" Ed bellowed over the engine.

Ali ignored him, working the steering wheel in an attempt to gain momentum. Through the branches she spotted a clearing. With a thump from behind her ATV's nose lifted. She didn't need to turn to know that the driver had jumped from his vehicle onto the back of hers.

As the Polaris burst out of the bushes into another clearing she gunned the engine, swinging the wheel from side to side. They fishtailed across wet grass, the knobby tires throwing up plumes of mud.

"Stop the damn buggy."

She felt a hand grab at her hair and ducked forward. Through the trees ahead she spotted the river.

Ali gave the thousand cc engine its head.

"Fucking stop!" screamed Ed as he clung to the roll cage.

"Go to hell."

At the last safe moment she spun the wheel and jammed on the brakes. Her intent was to throw the man into the river. However, she didn't anticipate the slick grass.

The Polaris spun like a top, flinging the man clear. With the engine still racing it flipped and rolled down the embankment, tumbling into the river.

Ali clung to the steering wheel as the Polaris dropped through the cold clear water. It hit the rocky bottom upside down and rolled with the current, coming to a halt against a submerged log. She didn't panic until she tried to leave the cabin and found her foot wedged under the accelerator.

With water pushing against her she couldn't free her

hiking boot. She lost her grip and the flow of the river grabbed her, twisting her torso out of the cabin. Panic escalated as she fought the current, her foot trapped. Her lungs burned, her injured arm screamed with pain as she desperately tried to pull her leg free. She spun back and forth, wriggling her toes in one last futile attempt to break free.

Blackness filled the edges of her vision as she looked up through the water at the light above. It was so close and yet so distant. Then, as she felt her strength ebb her foot slipped from the boot and she was free.

Her head broke the surface in a maelstrom of white water. She sucked in a lungful of air before being pulled back under. Managing to roll onto her back she lifted her legs and rode the rapids.

Minutes later the river calmed and she was able to swim to the bank. Lying on a pebbly beach she sucked air into her aching lungs. She allowed herself only a moment's rest before climbing to her feet and checking her surroundings.

She'd floated at least half a mile downstream from where the buggy had sunk. That was faster than she could move on foot. The river was her best chance of getting help, quickly.

At the far end of the beach she spotted a plastic drum wedged in a pile of debris. Digging it out she checked the lid was tight and waded out into the freezing water with it clutched to her chest. When her feet left the bottom she let the current grab her and she floated downstream.

With the sun low on the horizon it wouldn't be long before it disappeared completely, taking with it the last traces of warmth. Already she could feel the river sapping her body's heat. She needed to find help before she succumbed to the cold.

As Ali fought hypothermia, Rick and Jenny were dealing with the other end of the spectrum. The pair was drenched in sweat and short of breath as they took a break so Rick could orientate himself to the ground.

"We're close to the plantation. I remember this tree." The SEAL pointed to a pine that had been split by lightning.

Jenny waited patiently as he scanned the terrain. Axe sat by her side, watching with his head cocked.

He pointed to a thick grove of trees. "This way."

They set off and a moment later the dense underbrush parted revealing rows of planted marijuana.

Jenny looked up at the camouflage netting strung in the trees. "Holy crap. They've been growing this right under our noses."

"Pretty slick little setup. Must be a couple of thousand plants under here. I wouldn't be surprised if there are more plantations spread out in the forest."

She nodded. "Could be. Apart from a few ATV operators no one comes out here. They usually camp at Granite Hut and then head west into the park."

"That's why Carter and his buddies chose this spot."

"So what do you think? Should we wait for Ali's help to arrive?"

"No, might be too late. We're going to free the guys, but before we do that we need to even the numbers a little."

"Lure them out?"

"Yep, and into a trap."

"Do you have something in mind?"

He frowned. "Not really. I was hoping we might crack it together."

"Teamwork, yeah I think we'll be able to come up with something." She shot him a coy smile.

There was a moment as they stared at each other. Jenny caught herself thinking about how good his lips would feel pressed against hers.

"Right." He broke eye contact. "What gear do we have?" Rick emptied the contents of his backpack. There was a water bladder, a roll of tape, gas cylinders, a coil of nylon rope and ammunition.

Jenny did likewise adding more rope, a hand saw, bivy sack, small shovel, fire starters, medical kit, toilet paper and some rations.

They both sat silently staring at the gear.

"OK, MacGyver, I think I've got an idea," said Jenny.

"Good, because all I've come up with is an exploding toilet paper bomb."

Ali could no longer feel her hands and feet as she kicked ashore, released the drum and crawled up onto the beach. She lay there for a moment, gathering herself before she managed to climb shakily to her feet.

The sun had set and the light was fading as she climbed the riverbank. She recognized the park from where they had waited for the raft the day prior. Remembering the way to the road she hugged her arms around her body and hobbled toward it.

She waited beside the road for ten minutes without a car appearing. Shivering uncontrollably she started walking in the direction of the ranger station.

It wasn't long till a flash of headlights warned her of an approaching vehicle.

She stood in the middle of the road waving her arms. A pickup stopped with a screech of tires.

A door opened and an agitated voice yelled out at her, "What the hell are you doing in the middle of the road, woman? I could have killed you."

Ali staggered toward the truck. "I need help. I just came off the river. My friends are in trouble."

The elderly driver was a sixth generation mountain man and immediately recognized the onset of hypothermia. He grabbed his jacket from the truck, threw it over her shoulders and bundled her into the cab. Moments later, with the heater blazing they drove toward town.

"I'm going to get you to the hospital."

"No, no," Ali managed through teeth chattering like a machine gun. "My friends need help. Please, take me to the ranger station."

He frowned. "You sure? Those lips of yours are pretty blue."

She nodded.

He reached across and popped the glove compartment. "Have a look in there. Should be something to keep you warm."

She found a hip flask nestled among dog-eared manuals and paperwork.

"Best bourbon in Oregon."

She unscrewed the lid, gave it a sniff and took a sip. The smooth liquid warmed her throat and then her stomach. "Thank you."

"Tom, name's Tom."

"I'm Ali."

"Pleasure to meet you, Ali. Now, we're about twenty minutes from the ranger station. How's about you tell me what happened to you and your friends."

Ali took another sip then began the story.

Darkness had set in early under the thick forest canopy. Working more by touch than sight Rick hauled on a rope, looped it around a branch, pulled it tight and tied it off. "That's a wrap."

"Impressive," said Jenny from the darkness. "Let's hope it works."

Rick made his way across to where she was consolidating their supplies. Axe sat next to her, watching intently.

"No reason it shouldn't. Your plan is good."

She handed him a granola bar. "I think your knots are the key."

He unwrapped the snack. "Knots are all I've got. I'm a SEAL out of water."

"You've done pretty well so far," she murmured as she glanced up at the sky. "Rick, it's getting dark. Should we wait for morning?"

"Yeah, I was thinking we attack at the crack of dawn. They'll be up all night, tired and more likely to make mistakes." He chewed the bar.

"Makes sense." Jenny opened a packet of jerky and fed some of it to Axe. "How long have you been in the navy?"

"Twelve years now. I started in the fleet and moved across to the SEALs about eight years ago. What about you? How long have you been a ranger?"

She offered him a piece. "Not long."

He waved it away. "Axe needs it more than me."

"I was a lawyer in New York, hated it. Threw it all in to move out here and become a ranger."

"And part-time pole dancing instructor slash torture consultant."

She laughed. "Yeah, that too."

"So, is there a man in your life?"

"No, I left a guy in New York. Not about to go jumping back into a relationship. What about you?"

"I got married a few years back."

Jenny felt disappointment wash over her.

"Worst decision of my life. It lasted a little over eight months. Fortunately, we didn't have kids."

Axe let out a sigh as he lay next to Jenny. She turned and ruffled his ears, hiding her smile. "Too much time away?"

"No, she wasn't a good match for me. TJ would call it a poor life choice."

"Is TJ your boss?"

"Yeah, he's in that cage with the rest of my team. Best friends a guy could have."

"Ali said you guys were a tight crew."

"She's part of the family. Even passed selection."

"Selection?"

Rick's teeth flashed in the darkness. "You know, we should get some sleep. It's going to be an early one."

Jenny pulled a Gore-Tex bivy and a sleeping bag from her backpack and passed them to Rick. "I'll keep the first watch."

"No need. Axe has the best nose and ears in the business. Anyone comes within a hundred yards and he'll wake us. I'll take the bivy. You'll stay warmer in the sleeping bag."

"That thing's not going to keep you warm."

"It's OK. I'll snuggle with Axe."

"Don't be silly. The best way to conserve body heat is to

share it. Stuff the bag full of pine needles, it will insulate us from the ground.

Rick did as he was told and when the bag was full he handed it to Jenny who laid it on the ground. Then she unzipped the sleeping bag. "Sorry, you're going to have to be the big spoon."

"I've got to warn you," said Rick as he placed his shotgun within arm's reach, "I smell pretty bad." He lay and Jenny wiggled in front of him. Axe lay alongside her.

"Hey, at least you're not wearing that wetsuit anymore."

He draped the sleeping bag over her.

Jenny was overcome with a sense of well-being. She felt safe lying next to Rick. It was a sensation she'd never experienced with her ex.

A strong arm reached over and pulled her in tight. She could smell his sweat mixed with the damp of the forest. A smile formed on her lips as she realized this was the first time she'd laid with a man since moving to Oregon.

"Are you comfortable," he asked softly.

"Yeah, the smell isn't too bad. What about you?"

"Remarkably so."

There was a moment's silence. It was Rick who broke it. "Brown bears, mild concussions, gunfights, hostages and shotgun-toting yokels aside, this has been a very rewarding trip. I sure am glad I met you, Jenny."

"Let's keep it professional," she murmured as she drifted off to sleep.

"Yes, ma'am."

———————

Less than half a mile away inside Travis's cabin Carter had assembled his men. Ed, Harold, Hank and Carl, with his arm bandaged, sat around the table. Travis had been relegated to guarding the prisoners.

"So, let me get this straight. You idiots let an unarmed man, two women and a dog get the better of you?" growled Carter.

"One of the women drowned," said Hank.

"Oh, that makes this so much better." Carter fixed him with a steely glare. "That SEAL bastard and that bitch, Jenny, are still out there. I want them found."

Ed frowned. "Boss, we go out there now and we're going to blunder around in the darkness till we run into them." He gestured to Hank and Carl. "And, thanks to these two they've got guns."

He considered the point. "We go at first light." He turned to Hank. "That hound of yours going to be any use?"

"He can track them, but we need to put a bullet in that mongrel of theirs."

"Well, I'm sure between the four of you, it won't be a problem. Travis and I will hold the fort. I've got two of my deputies patrolling the main road in case they try to make a run for it. They'll hand 'em over no questions asked."

"They'll have to walk out. I fixed that ranger's truck good," said Harold.

Carter nodded. "There are only two of them, they've got no comms and they don't know this area like we do. It shouldn't take you long to wrap them up. Get some sleep. We roll at dawn."

"You want us to swap with Travis?" asked one of the men.

"No, that slug has been sitting on his ass all day. I'll take over from him in a few hours."

"And the prisoners?"

"Tomorrow they go in the river, with or without their buddies. Then we'll harvest the crop, burn this place to the ground and get the hell out of here."

"Why don't we burn them with the cabin?" suggested Hank.

Carter's lip turned up in a sinister smile. "Yeah, I like that idea. Fire will rip through this area. By the time they find the bodies we'll be long gone."

"That means we can shoot the nigger and the girl?" asked Ed.

He nodded. "And the mongrel. Kill all three of 'em."

———

Maria poured fresh coffee into Leonie's cup and patted her shoulder. "It's going to be OK."

"We haven't heard from them in…" She glanced up at the digital clock on the wall. "Five hours. Something has happened. We need to get a search party out there, right now."

Ben, the ranger, looked up from his workstation. "The search party's heading out at first light. You shouldn't worry. The radio probably went down at Granite Hut. It can be a bit patchy. I wouldn't be surprised if Jenny has them all there."

"I shouldn't worry? My kid sister's out there along with her fiancé, their dog, Maria's husband and the rest of their team. If something's happened to them I won't be able to live with myself."

"We're doing everything we can," said Maria as she offered the pot of coffee to Ben.

Leonie sighed and turned her attention back to the

computer monitor that showed all the incoming communications traffic. The last message from Ali at Granite Hut had been received at lunchtime.

An alarm chimed telling them that someone had opened the front door. Leonie glanced at the monitor that displayed a video feed from the reception area. She instantly recognized her sister wrapped in a jacket. There was a man with her. She leaped from her chair. "It's Ali!"

Dashing through the office she burst into the waiting area and wrapped her sister in a hug. "Oh god, I thought I'd lost you." She immediately noticed how cold Ali was. "Maria, we need coffee and blankets."

She bundled Ali through to the living area at the back of the station and sat her on a bunk.

Maria appeared with a pile of blankets and piping hot coffee. "Let's get her out of those damp clothes."

Ali waved them away. "No, first we need to contact Commander Conner."

Ernie's wife frowned. "Why? What's happened?"

"The boys have been captured by drug growers. They're being held in a cabin in the hills." Ali took a sip of coffee.

Leonie's eyebrows rose. "You're kidding me?"

She shook her head. "No, they flipped their raft. Tried to walk out and ran into a dope plantation. Rick and Jenny are still up there. We need to get them help."

"Seriously, those boys could stir up trouble in a cemetery." Leonie turned and bellowed through the open door, "Ben, we've got ourselves a situation. I'm going to need a direct line to the DEA."

"I'll call Conner," said Maria. "You get a warm shower. Jenny's locker is over there. Her clothes should fit. Don't you worry about any of this, Leonie and I will sort it out."

Ali followed them into the command room and watched

as the two women snapped into action. Suddenly over-whelmed with fatigue, she sat in a chair and sipped her coffee. Finally, she felt like she could rest. Help for Mike and the others was on the way.

Chapter Fourteen

Jenny's lips felt soft and warm as they pressed against Rick's cheek. He sighed turning his head until he could kiss her full on the mouth. Her tongue pressed against his then ran its way across his face leaving a wet trail. "What the hell?"

His eyes darted open as Axe's whiskers tickled his nostrils. The kiss had been a dream. All except the part with the tongue. He shoved the dog away. "Thanks, bud."

He remembered he was lying next to Jenny and gently eased himself away so he could wipe his face and check his watch. It was a little after five in the morning.

"Good morning," said Jenny as she sat up.

"Sleep well?" he asked.

"Surprisingly." She gathered up the bedding, emptied out the leaves and stuffed it back into her pack.

Rick rose and checked the traps they'd built the night before. Everything was still intact. He picked up the shotgun and rifle then shouldered his backpack. "You ready for this?"

Jenny handed her pistol to him and checked her shotgun. "Let's do it."

They followed Axe through the woods until they reached the edge of the drug plantation. The sun was rising casting a soft glow across the crop.

"You sure about this?" he asked. "I can do it alone."

She turned and placed a hand on the side of his face. Leaning in she kissed him softly.

For a moment Rick was somewhere other than the drug plantation. The location was irrelevant, all that existed was the taste and feel of her lips and mouth.

"We're a team now," she said when they parted. "Now, let's rescue your friends."

He grinned. "Fuck yeah."

She kissed him again. "Get into position."

Rick left her at the edge of the plantation and made his way between the rows of waxen green plants. He felt elated, partially because of the pending action, but mostly because Jenny liked him. He felt like a teenager giddy with first love as he stalked through the marijuana crop. Pausing he exhaled and focused. This wasn't about him. This was about freeing Mike and the boys and then exacting a little revenge on the criminals holding them.

***

Harold and Ed led the hunting party. Hank, without his dog, and Carl, with his arm bandaged, had been relegated to supporting roles. The four men left the cabin at first light armed to the teeth with shotguns, pistols and two AR-15 assault rifles. Ed had a walkie-talkie attached to his belt.

"We'll skirt the plantation," said Ed as they paused at

the edge of the clearing. "Harold can track a field mouse through a parking lot. Shouldn't take us long to pick up their trail and run them down."

"What if they legged it out of the park?" asked Hank.

"Then our buddies would have picked them up. Damn, do you two just play stupid or are you actually thick as shit," snapped Ed.

Harold stood peering into the forest as his partner ripped into the other men. "Guys, I think I see something." He pointed through the bushes.

Ed raised his AR-15 and peered through the scope. In the soft morning light he spotted something fluttering in the breeze. "This way." He gestured for the others to follow.

The four men moved swiftly into the thick undergrowth that bordered the camouflaged plantation. Harold took the lead, scanning the soft ground for footprints.

He found a food wrapper stuck in the branches of a bush. Plucking it free he rolled the plastic between his fingers and sniffed it. "This is new." He dropped to a knee and examined the ground. A trail of boot marks led into the forest. "They went this way."

The path their prey had taken became even clearer to the tracker as they moved deeper into the woods. His experienced eye was drawn to broken twigs, scuff marks in the leaves and indentations in the soft soil.

Ed was the first to spot their quarry. "Down there," he whispered, gesturing through a gap in the trees. A figure was walking slowly away from them. It disappeared into a thick patch of bushes.

Weapons held ready they gave chase, sliding through the leaf litter that covered the steep slope.

Ed spotted their target again, long brown hair and a

feminine build revealing it was the park ranger. She turned, saw them and started running.

A weapon fired alongside his ear and a bullet blew a chunk out of a tree.

"What the fuck!" Ed screamed at Hank who held the smoking rifle. "It's just the girl. If we bring her in alive Carter might let us have some fun with her."

Harold pushed ahead, sprinting through the scrub like a dog on the scent of a rabbit. Ed wasn't far behind his eyes peeled for any sign of the SEAL or the dog.

"She's on her own," hollered his partner.

They covered a hundred yards through thick under-growth, closing the gap between them and the girl. She wore a backpack, but as far as Ed could see she was unarmed. He raised his AR-15 in the air and fired.

Terrified the girl slipped, fell to the ground and clam-bered back to her feet.

"Hold it right there sweetheart!" yelled Ed.

She was a dozen feet in front of them when she stopped and turned. "Please don't hurt me."

Ed eyeballed the empty holster on her belt as he came up alongside Harold, who had her covered with his shotgun. "Where's your SEAL buddy?"

Hank and Carl caught up, skidding to a halt behind them.

"He went for help," she managed through her tears.

The four men stood in a semi-circle not more than ten feet from their quarry. Like a pack of hyenas confronting a lioness they tentatively edged forward. Ed's eyes darted from side to side as he searched for any sign of the SEAL or the dog.

The ranger swayed slightly, reached out and grasped a tree.

Hank lowered his weapon. "She looks like she's gonna faint."

She pulled at something and suddenly a rope snaked through the leaves alongside them. Ed frowned as his eyes followed it. Then a noise behind him caught his attention. He turned at the same time as the others.

"Fuck," was all he managed as a three hundred pound log swung down toward them. It hit Carl and Hank with a sickening crunch as he dove sideways. The two men and log slammed into Harold, knocking him off his feet. It caught Ed a glancing blow sending him sprawling, his rifle flung from his hands.

He hit the ground with a thud, pain shooting up from a bruised thigh. He rolled over to see the park ranger standing over the crumpled heap of the other three men with a pump action shotgun in her shoulder.

"You fucking whore," he said as he reached for his rifle.

A savage growl filled the air and he froze. He found himself staring directly into the bared fangs of a mean looking dog.

"I wouldn't move if I were you," said the ranger. "That's a trained attack dog. One word from me and he'll tear out your throat." She tossed something into his lap.

He glanced at the roll of tape and then at the men lying under the suspended log. Hank and Carl were out cold. Harold stared silently into the barrel of her shotgun.

She flashed him a smile. "Now, how about you crawl over here real slowly and tape up your buddies."

"How about you go to hell."

The dog let out a loud bark and another savage growl.

"Pardon me?"

Ed swallowed, picked up the tape and slid slowly across

to the others. The dog followed him its eyes locked on his throat.

Behind him in the leaves, his radio hissed. "Ed, what the hell's going on down there?" demanded Carter.

Chapter Fifteen

Rick's adrenaline was firing, his heart pounding as he sprinted through the marijuana plants in the direction of the ambush. He'd heard a single gunshot and then nothing, a sure sign that Jenny was in trouble.

As he reached the edge of the plantation another shot rang out followed by a second and a third. He skidded to a halt and exhaled. That was the signal he'd given her. The ambush had been a success. Now, he could focus on rescuing the team.

He made his way back through the plantation, searching for his backpack. Locating it he rummaged inside and removed a gas stove and spare canister. Placing the burner under a plant he lit it and sat the canister on top.

Leaving the bag he continued through the plantation with the lever action rifle in one hand and the shotgun in the other. He had Jenny's Glock stuffed into the back of his shorts.

Reaching the edge of the marijuana plants he slid to his stomach and crawled forward till he could see the cabin.

He was on the opposite side to the cage that held his friends. Between them were the porch and two ATVs. An overweight figure sat in a rocking chair with a shotgun across his knees watching the cage. Rick lined him up with the rifle.

A second figure appeared from the cabin. This guy was tall with a Stetson, cowboy boots and a pistol belt. He stormed across to the cage and aimed his pistol at the group of captives. Rick assumed that this was Carter, the guy in charge.

"I know you're out there," he bellowed. "Show yourself or I'm going to start killing your buddies."

Rick didn't have a shot from where he was lying and if he did and missed it could hit the others. What's more he didn't have much faith in the old lever action's accuracy.

"I'm not messing around. You've got five seconds before I shoot this old bastard in the face," bellowed the man.

Rick contemplated calling his bluff. However, something told him that Carter had the will to kill TJ.

"Four."

He dropped the rifle and stood.

"Three."

He walked slowly toward the cabin.

"Two."

The fat bastard on the porch nearly fell out of his chair. "He's here! Carter, he's here!" he said as he stood and aimed his shotgun.

Carter turned as Rick stopped alongside the ATVs. "Travis, you got him covered?" he asked.

"Yeah, he as much as smiles and I'll blow his head off."

Carter holstered his pistol and took a pair of handcuffs from his belt. "Where are the woman and the dog?" He tossed them onto the ground in front of Rick.

"I don't know."

"Sure you don't. Put the damn cuffs on."

As Rick bent down to retrieve the handcuffs there was a loud explosion in the plantation; the gas canister. He dropped to one knee, snatched the Glock from the back of his shorts and aimed it at Carter.

A shotgun boomed from the porch. He barely registered the sting in his buttocks as pellets ripped into his flesh.

Carter dove for cover as Rick fired rapidly. His shots struck a pile of drums where he had disappeared.

Movement near the cage caught his eye and he spotted Jenny emerging from the marijuana her shotgun held ready, Axe by her side.

The report of a gun reminded him that Travis, the fat bastard, was still on the porch. He popped up over the ATV and snapped off a shot hitting him in the torso. The morbidly obese redneck didn't flinch and racked his shotgun. "I'm a gonna kill you."

Rick heard a pistol shot and felt the bullet crease his shoulder as he fired another round into Travis. He spun and saw Carter running toward one of the other ATVs. Jenny's shotgun boomed and buckshot impacted the ground around the man as he leaped into the vehicle. Rick tried to raise the Glock but his arm was unresponsive.

Jenny fired again and pellets sprayed the ATV as it started and took off with a roar. Axe sprinted after it, barking frantically.

Rick checked to see that Travis was down as he climbed into the remaining buggy.

"Shove over big boy," said Jenny as she made to jump into the driver's seat.

He grinned and slid sideways, transferring his pistol to

his good arm. A glance in the wing mirror confirmed that she had freed Mike and the others.

Jenny gunned the ATV and sent it power sliding around the corner. He was impressed; she handled the powerful buggy like a rally driver. In a matter of seconds, they'd caught up with Axe.

Rick let out a whistle and the dog pulled to one side of the road. Jenny slowed and he leaped onto the rear seats. "Good boy," said Rick as the dog licked him. "Now, let's get this Carter dickhead."

Jenny floored the throttle and sent the Polaris soaring over a rise in the road.

As they landed with a bounce Rick spotted Carter's buggy ahead. He gripped the handle in front of him with his bad hand and clutched the pistol with the other. "I'm going to shoot out his tires."

As she closed the gap between the two ATVs Rick fired a volley of bullets. They went wide. He tried again, striking the tailgate.

Hearing the shots Carter swerved his buggy from side to side, kicking up dust. Jenny closed the gap to a few feet. In the maelstrom of dust Rick couldn't get a clear shot.

"Hold on!" Jenny said as she rammed the back of Carter's ATV.

The impact jolted him forward and he braced himself, wounded shoulder burning. Then he felt Axe jump from the rear seat past his head onto the hood of the buggy. With a flash of fur he disappeared through the dust, leaping into the back of Carter's ATV.

Brake lights flashed and they slammed into the buggy again. Jenny fought to keep control as they skidded.

Carter's screams filled the air as his ATV slowed, angled off the track and bumped into a large tree.

Rick jumped out pistol in hand. As the dust cleared he saw Carter's predicament.

Axe had the crooked policeman by the back of his neck, his teeth sunk into the shirt collar. Fortunately for the military working dog the crooked cop had also lost his pistol. It lay out of reach in the foot well on the passenger side.

"I don't think he likes you," said Rick as he aimed the Glock.

"Get him off me. Please, get him off me," whimpered Carter.

Rick ordered the dog to release and gestured for Carter to climb out. "On your knees, hands behind your back."

Jenny produced a pair of handcuffs and soon Carter was sitting cuffed in the back of their buggy with Axe sitting alongside him, teeth bared.

"Way to go, sailor." Jenny gave his hand a squeeze.

He reached out, grasped her waist and pulled her in close. "Hey, it was all you, ranger girl."

They locked eyes for a moment and then Rick tipped his head forward and they touched lips. He forgot the pain in his shoulder and the pellets in his buttocks and legs as her mouth parted and they kissed long and hard.

Her body felt firm and muscular pressed against him as their tongues touched. Blood rushed to his groin and he felt it harden against her stomach.

"Steady on big boy," she murmured as their lips parted, "you're injured, remember."

As he held her he heard a faint yet familiar sound. The dull thud of helicopter blades grew louder. They both looked skyward as a black chopper thundered overhead.

"The cavalry has arrived," said Rick.

Jenny kissed him again. "No, our backup has arrived."

Rick laughed. "Good point. Shall we get back and see how the boys are doing?"

When they pulled up outside the cabin a squad of camouflaged operatives met them. A DEA team had rappelled in from the helicopter and secured the site.

Mike, Dean, Ernie and the Chief all sat on the porch drinking beers they'd raided from Travis's stash. The overweight pot grower was lying bandaged on a stretcher under the watchful eye of a DEA paramedic.

Axe leaped from the ATV and made a beeline for Mike. He knocked him backward spilling his beer as he licked his face. "Hey buddy, good to see you too," Mike said with a laugh.

All four men rose as Rick stepped from the ATV. Ernie was the first to reach him. The Latino threw his arms around his SEAL teammate. "You came through, bro. I thought we were dead. Then you come out all guns blazing like Rambo."

"I had help. Jenny's the one who found me."

Ernie looked confused. "You mean you had to find a pole-dancing instructor to save us."

Rick elbowed him. "She's a park ranger."

Ernie shook his head. "No, essé, she's a hero." He ran across and embraced the ranger.

Mike shook his hand next. "Thanks, brother."

"That dog of yours. He's pretty damn amazing."

Mike nodded in the direction of Jenny. "Pretty good matchmaker too." He headed over to thank the ranger.

"Looks like you learned something out there," said TJ as he approached.

"Yeah, I learned I'm sticking to boats. This forest crap is bullshit."

TJ placed a hand on his shoulder. "And here's me thinking you'd found a little humility." He grinned. "You did good, son. We'll make a woodsman out of you yet."

Dean was the last to offer his thanks to Rick. Then they all retired to the porch to drink beers as the DEA team secured Carter and his cronies. Jenny found a medical kit and inspected Rick's wounds between sips of her ale.

"Hey Rick," said Ernie. "How come you're the one who always gets shot?"

"Because, unlike you I'm not small enough to hide behind every bit of cover."

"That's so racist," declared the Latino.

"How is calling you a midget racist?" Rick winced as Jenny applied a dressing to his shoulder.

"Rick's right. He's a heightist," said the Chief.

"Well, if you didn't work out so much there wouldn't be so much of you to get shot," quipped Ernie.

Jenny snickered as she finished bandaging his wound.

"Oh, you think he's funny?"

She shook her head. "I think you're all crazy. Do you have many adventures like this?"

"Too many," lamented Mike. "From now on TJ is banned from planning any group activities outside of work."

"Amen to that," echoed Ernie and Rick.

As they laughed and drank one of the DEA agents approached. "Guys, we've prepared a landing zone a little way up the road. If you take the ATV's up there the helicopter will be able to lift you out to the ranger station. There's a paramedic team waiting there for you."

The Chief raised his beer. "Thanks, bud."

Mike was the first off the chopper when it touched down in a field behind the ranger station. With Axe by his side he ran straight into the arms of Ali, who was waiting with Maria and Leonie.

"I'm so sorry, babe. You must have been worried to death."

She nodded with eyes filled with tears. "Yes, I was."

He hugged her again and then she knelt and wrapped her arms around Axe. "I don't know what I would do without you, bud. You're the only thing keeping everyone in this family alive."

Axe licked the side of her face and wagged his tail furiously.

"That dog's a damn good SEAL," said TJ as he and the rest of the team joined them. Ernie already had his arms wrapped around his wife.

"OK team," said Ali's sister. "Maria and I have whipped up some coffee and breakfast inside. If you've got any injuries you should head over and see the medics." She pointed to the ambulance parked a dozen yards away.

"You're unbelievable, Leonie," said Ali.

She shrugged. "It's nothing. I mean, as of next week all you special kids are going to be family. Like it or not I'm lumped with you."

Jenny laughed as she helped Rick limp across to the back of the ambulance.

"It's a pretty crazy family," he said as one of the medics pulled out a stretcher and he eased himself up onto it.

"They're a pretty tight bunch," she said. "You're lucky to have friends like that." She turned to the medic. "He's got a gunshot graze to the right shoulder and buckshot wounds to the buttocks and legs."

"Got it, make yourself comfortable, sir."

Rick lay down with a pillow under his face.

"How's our hero?" he heard TJ ask.

"He'll be okay once the medic pulls the buckshot out of his butt," replied Jenny.

"Can I have some goddamn privacy?" bellowed Rick.

"Sure thing." The medic slid the gurney into the back of the ambulance. "Is the lady allowed to stay?"

"Yeah, someone has to hold my hand."

The doors of the van closed and Jenny sat opposite.

"You attached to these shorts?" asked the medic.

"Not particularly," replied Rick. He jolted as the medic used shears to cut away his shorts and underwear. "Steady there, bud."

"You've got a lovely butt," Jenny said with a chuckle. "Well except for the buckshot."

He felt the medic examining his wounds with a metal probe.

"What are you doing next Wednesday?" he asked.

"Look, we just met," quipped the medic.

Rick shook his head.

"I'm not sure, why?" responded Jenny.

"I need a date for Mike and Ali's wedding."

"You're asking me to go to your teammate's wedding with you? Isn't that kind of a big deal?"

He turned and smiled. "Yeah, it is."

She leaned forward and kissed him. "I'd love to go."

"Sir, this might hurt a little."

Rick felt a sharp pain in his buttocks as the medic used a pair of forceps to pluck shot from the flesh. "Son of a bitch."

He twitched as the wound was squirted with antiseptic then sponged dry and dressed. "You're real lucky these didn't go very deep."

"That's what she said," joked Rick as the medic removed another pellet. "Holy shit. What are you doing back there?"

Jenny kissed him on the side of the face. "Come on. I thought you were a big tough SEAL."

His eyes narrowed. "And I thought you were a sensitive park ranger."

A wicked smile flashed across her face. "You've got a lot to learn." Then she turned to the medic. "Any chance I can take over?"

Chapter Sixteen

A little over a week later and Rick, TJ, Ernie and Dean sat in a row of chairs in a picturesque vineyard nestled in the rugged hills of Swartz Canyon, San Diego. All four were dressed in dark blue suits with matching silver ties.

In front of them under a vine covered arbor adorned with flowers stood Mike. Dressed in a tailored tuxedo he wore a smile a mile wide. Next to him sat Axe, his coat freshly groomed and a bowtie fitted to his collar.

Mike turned and Rick shot him a broad smile and a wink. A feeling of pride swelled through his chest as his teammate waited for his bride to be.

Glancing over his shoulder he spotted Jenny sitting with Leonie and Maria. His date looked beautiful in a silver dress with an exposed back. She wore her hair high with sprigs of white flowers in it. He grinned, she looked more elegant than any woman he'd ever laid eyes on.

She caught his eye and smiled. It was the look that a woman reserved for the man she loved. It was subtle, but

Rick felt it like a hit of morphine. A warm sensation flooded his body and he smiled back.

Suddenly, music filled the air and he rose with the others. Everyone turned to face the red carpet that ran from the lush green vines between the rows of chairs to the altar.

Ali stepped into view on her father's arm and the crowd let out a collective sigh. She looked stunning in a simple yet elegant off-the-shoulder dress that barely touched the ground. Like Jenny she wore her hair up, except hers was adorned with white roses.

He turned back to Mike and saw the look of pure bliss on his SEAL buddy's face. A little over a week ago he wouldn't have truly understood how Mike felt, but since meeting Jenny that had changed. "He looks so happy," he whispered.

Ernie gave a quiet chuckle. "Bro, you haven't seen the shit eating grin on your face."

He frowned. "What's that supposed to mean?"

"It means you're in love, essé."

Rick leaned down so his mouth was close to Ernie's ear. "You might be right, but if you tell anyone I'm going to kick your ass."

He straightened up as Ali's father passed her across to Mike. Then a priest joined the two of them.

The service was short and sweet. Axe supplied the ring. Then the priest declared them man and wife. They kissed and cheers filled the vineyard.

While the newlyweds and Axe disappeared for photos the wedding guests, under the guidance of Leonie, gathered inside the winery for drinks.

Rick and Jenny joined Ernie, Maria and TJ at the bar.

"What a beautiful wedding," said Jenny.

"Ali looked amazing," added Maria.

The boys ordered beers and stepped away leaving the ladies talking.

The Chief raised his beer. "So, Rick. The last man standing."

"Once stung, twice shy," he replied.

"You seem pretty smitten with your ranger," said TJ.

"You're in love, bro," added Ernie.

Rick shrugged. "Maybe." He took a sip of his beer.

TJ grinned. "Maybe? Maybe it's time to run another Girlfriend Selection Course."

Rick snorted into his beer. It sprayed froth over the three others. "Nope. I ain't doing that shit." He coughed up amber liquid.

Jenny and Maria glanced over.

TJ laughed, relieving Rick of the overflowing beer. "Relax. I think it's safe to say that Jenny can skip selection. I mean hell, she rescued our asses."

Ernie stepped over to the bar and grabbed another beer.

"What am I, chopped liver?" said Rick.

Ernie handed him a bottle. "Hey, we know you helped out. You make a pretty good sidekick."

Rick glared as the girls joined them and Jenny kissed his cheek. "What are you boys talking about?"

TJ smiled. "We were just reminiscing about how Mike and Ali met. Rick was saying how much he enjoyed the selection course."

She grinned. "Oh, yes. He mentioned that up in Oregon, but never got to explain it."

Maria grasped her by the arm. "That's not a story you want to hear without champagne."

As Ernie's wife directed her back to the bar Jenny

flashed Rick a smile. He returned it staring intensely into her eyes.

"Oh, she's got you bad," TJ said.

"Signed SEAL'd and delivered," added Ernie. "This time next year we'll be doing it all over."

"If, and I mean if I ever get married again, there will be no bachelor party, no secret plans and no damn shenanigans."

TJ lifted his beer. "Here's to shenanigans."

It was well after three in the morning when Rick and Jenny arrived at the villa he'd rented a short Uber ride from the wedding venue. As he fumbled with the front door he felt Jenny's arms around his waist.

"You look so damn handsome in that suit," she murmured as her lips caressed his ear.

He abandoned the door, turned and met her lips with his own. The kiss was long, passionate and sent fire coursing through his veins.

When, after minutes their lips finally parted Rick was breathing heavily. "You, you're something else Jenny. I've never met a woman like you before."

She grinned, her hands traveling from his waist to his groin where she squeezed him gently through the fabric of his suit. "So, you think I could pass your selection course?"

His brow rose. "Ah, Maria spilled the beans."

"Yes, she also told me I'm the first woman to tame the untamable Rick."

"Tame me? That's fun–"

She squeezed him again and pressed her mouth against

his. They kissed like teenagers as she unzipped his fly and slipped her hand inside his pants.

He let out a soft moan and moved his lips to her neck as he slid the thin straps of her dress over her shoulders and unzipped the satin material. The garment slid to her waist revealing her pert breasts.

"Are you going to do something about the door," she murmured. "Or are we going to make love on the porch."

It took Rick a matter of seconds to open it.

Jenny stepped inside, pushed her dress down her hips and let it slide to the floor. She stepped out of it and walked slowly along the hall in just her panties and heels.

Rick stood in the doorway his eyes glued to her lithe body.

She glanced back at him. "You going to stand there gawking or come in?"

"Huh, yeah." He closed the door, shrugged off his jacket and followed her into the bedroom.

She lay back on the bed as he shed his clothes. His eyes never left hers as she watched him intently.

When he was completely naked she smiled. "God you're a hunk of a man." She beckoned with her finger.

He started at her feet. Softly kissing her legs, thighs, stomach and breasts, he slowly made his way up the bed. Finally, when their mouths touched he felt her hand grasp his manhood. She pushed aside her underwear and slowly guided him in as they kissed.

Epilogue

Vicente Barbosa sat on the plush mattress he'd had smuggled into his prison cell and studied the cards in his hand. The poker game had become something of a tradition. Every Friday three of the most influential men in the maximum-security facility joined him for a game.

On his immediate left sat Enrique a Hispanic gangbanger and mass murderer from MS13. Next to him was a hulking African American with a shaved head; Trey an enforcer from Detroit. The brute was rumored to have murdered an entire family with his bare hands. The third man, arguably the most influential in their current environment was Jules Deveron, the prison's head guard. At six-foot-five with the build of a professional wrestler he was a man who demanded and received the utmost respect from all but the stupidest of prisoners.

The guard pushed the last of his cigarettes into the center of the table and narrowed his eyes. "OK, Vicente. Show us your cards."

Barbosa shrugged and tossed his hand on the table, a pair of aces.

"You shitting me?" exclaimed Enrique. "Two lousy aces. You got balls essé. Big brass balls."

"Yeah, but balls or no balls that's still a shitty hand." Deveron tossed a straight flush on the table and grinned. "You can have the cigarettes, divvy them between yourselves." He rose from the plastic stool. "I've got to get back to my reports."

He made for the cell door where two of his guards were waiting. As he was about to leave he stopped and turned, reaching into his jacket. "Almost forgot. Mail for Mr. Barbosa." He tossed a letter toward the former cartel kingpin. "Same time next week, gentlemen. Stay out of trouble."

He disappeared and the guards gestured for Trey and Enrique to follow.

Barbosa waited until they were gone and his cell door locked before he opened the envelope.

The hand written letters were a coded report from his men in Mexico. They informed him of shipments, earnings, thefts and actions taken to remedy problems. He noted that profits were up; his second in command was doing well.

Among the reports was a letter from his wife. His son had made the state soccer team and his grades had improved.

The final item in the envelope was a single piece of paper with a photograph printed on it. The glossy shot was a wedding photo. A man and a woman stood in front of a priest with a dog by their side.

He sat staring at the picture, channeling hatred at the people and animal that had put him in this shit hole far from his family and his beloved Mexico.

Scrunching the paper into a ball he tossed it at the wall. "I'm going to destroy you, Michael Saunders. I'm going to wait till you have a family of your own and then you're going to watch them die."

Next in the SEAL Series

vinci-books.com/seal-signed-delivered

A Navy SEAL, his canine partner, and a cartel kingpin hellbent on revenge.

When a cartel kingpin seeks retribution, Navy SEAL Mike Saunders and his faithful hound Axe find themselves in the crosshairs. As their team leader, Chief TJ Lines, grapples with personal heartbreak, Mike must summon all his skills to protect the innocent and save Axe from a terrifying fate.

Turn the page for a free preview…

Signed SEAL'd and Delivered: Chapter One

Mike Saunders lay on a deck chair under a tree in the front yard of his house. A warm breeze rustled the leaves above as he stretched his muscled arms high and folded them behind his head. The corners of his mouth turned up in a smile and the edges of his grey eyes crinkled as he watched his son playing.

The two-year-old charged around the lawn with Axe, Mike's recently retired military working dog. The Belgian Malinois adored Junior and was closely supervising the toddler's activities.

Mike watched as Junior made a break toward his wife's rose bushes. Axe leaped into action, gently blocking his progress.

Junior clutched the dog's long fur, and the hound guided him back to the middle of the lawn. When the toddler was safe Axe sat on his haunches and looked toward Mike. One of his ears flopped over and his tongue lolled from the side of his mouth.

"Who needs a nanny when you've got Axe?" said a soft voice from behind.

He turned and watched his wife cross the lawn from the porch of their townhouse. Alison Saunders wore a floral print dress that hugged her curves, putting an even broader smile on his face.

His wife, a veterinarian, had bright green eyes, a button nose and plump lips that were perpetually turned up in a smile.

"What would we do without him?"

Ali reached the deck chair, hitched her dress and straddled him, leaning forward to kiss him. "Not as much of this."

Mike slipped his hands around her waist as she nibbled his lip. He felt the blood rush into his shorts as she ground down on him. "Spring is in the air?" he murmured.

Ali turned her attention to his ear, soft lips brushing the lobe. "It's a pity we've got an audience," she whispered.

Mike turned and looked directly into two pairs of bright inquisitive eyes. Both his son and dog were watching intently. "Isn't it time for Junior's nap?"

Ali nibbled his ear. "A huh, and if you put him to bed, we can have a nap of our own."

Mike slid his hands under her dress and along her thighs. "I'm heading out on an exercise. I'm not interested in napping."

She sat upright, shifting weight on to his crotch as she traced her fingers down his granite hard abs. "I suggest reading him *Bish the Adventure Jug*; it's his current favorite."

He groaned as she slid off him and walked toward the house. The dress did nothing to hide the lines of her butt as she climbed the porch. "Anytime now," she said with a chuckle as she disappeared inside.

Mike grinned to himself as he rose from the chair and crossed the lawn. He had to be one of the luckiest men alive, with a stunning wife, vibrant young son, great teammates and a killer job. He ruffled his dog's ears, a loyal best friend. Life was good.

Scooping his son from the grass he carried him toward the front door. As he reached for the handle, he sensed something was off and turned back to the yard.

Axe stood, staring past the rose bushes and through their white picket fence. Hackles raised and ears angled forward, it was body language that Mike knew from their time in combat.

"What's up boy?" Mike scanned the street as he bounced his son on his hip.

There were a half-dozen cars parked opposite, and he scanned each one. He spotted a white sedan in the shade of a leafy tree, and his eyes narrowed. Three years earlier, a similar car had played a role in the abduction and attempted murder of Ali. Shaking his head, he drove the idea from his mind; Barbosa was rotting in a maximum-security prison with eight life sentences.

Axe let out a half-hearted bark before joining him on the porch. The dog looked at him with intelligent brown eyes.

"What's up bud, squirrel?"

Axe cocked his head, and his right ear flopped forward. Mike reached down and ruffled his ears. Then he left the porch and walked through to Junior's bedroom. Axe's claws rattled on the floorboards as he followed. The toddler struggled to keep his eyes open as Mike tucked him into bed.

"Dadda, Axe," he managed between yawns.

"He's right here, bud." Mike kissed Junior on his forehead as the dog jumped onto the bed and curled up along-side his son.

He stroked Axe and kissed Junior again. Pausing a moment at the door, he smiled as his son reached out and placed one hand on the dog's paw. From the moment that Ali had introduced their son to his dog, the two had become inseparable. The former military working dog had taken it upon himself to watch over Junior and keep him safe.

"They're so cute," whispered his wife as she slipped an arm around his waist.

"Yeah." He turned and dipped his head to kiss her.

What started as a tender embrace rapidly escalated to heated passion as he maneuvered her into the hall. Items of clothing dropped to the floor as they continued along the passage into their bedroom. Mike removed her bra with a deft flick of his wrist and lifted her off the ground. She wrapped her legs around him as they kissed. Then he lowered her gently onto the bed.

"Can't TJ cancel the exercise so you can stay at home?" Ali purred.

Mike chuckled. "That ain't gonna happen. The old man spends all his time at the office."

"Trouble at home?"

He kissed her neck, gently brushing his lips against her skin. She moaned as he caressed her breasts. Slipping his fingers into the sides of her French cut briefs he slid them along her thighs as he continued kissing his way down her body.

Outside, less than fifty yards away in a white car, a man sat hunched over a tablet. On the seat next to him was a compact camera with a long lens.

On screen, he sorted through photos of Mike and his family as they relaxed in their yard. Selecting four images, he transferred them into an encrypted email account and hit send. Then he fished a phone from the pocket of his jacket. Holding the device to his mouth he recorded a message.

"I've sent you the pictures. Let me know what the next move is," he said in Spanish.

A moment later the message was sent and he awaited a reply. It came less than thirty seconds later in the form of text.

Maintain observation.

Ali took a sip from her coffee before slotting it into the cup holder on the handle of Junior's stroller. Her son was attached to his father's leg as Mike tossed a gear bag into the back of his pickup.

"Dadda, no go," he wailed.

Mike scooped him into his arms. "Hey bud, dad's got to go to work. I need you to stay here and look after mom and Axe."

"Nooo," he said shaking his head.

Ali thought her heart would break as her son buried his head into her husband's shoulder and clung to him like a koala. Feeling pressure against her leg she glanced down and saw that Axe was sitting alongside her. The dog had an uncanny knack for sensing emotions and offering support. She reached down and stroked his head.

"Hey bud, I gotta go look after my team. I'll only be gone a few days. Axe and mom need you here."

Axe barked, gaining Junior's attention, then jumped up on Mike so he could lick the boy's leg. The toddler's mood changed instantly. He giggled and reached for the dog's ears. "Dadda, down."

Mike lowered him, and he immediately wrapped his arms around Axe's neck.

"He's distracted, you need to go now," said Ali.

Mike nodded, stepped across and embraced her, kissing her softly. "I'll be back in a few days." Then he checked to make sure Axe and Junior were well clear of the pickup before jumping inside and pulling out of the drive. He gave Ali a wave as he drove away.

Once the truck had disappeared, she gathered her giggling son from the ground and placed him in the stroller. Axe stayed closed, continuing his role as the distractor.

"OK, boys. Let's get rolling."

Ali pushed the stroller across the lawn and out the gate. Axe fell in by her side. He was more than familiar with the routine of delivering Junior to daycare. The dog waited patiently as she secured the gate and handed her son a juice box. Then, with coffee in hand, they started the half-mile stroll.

For the last two months Ali had been working three half-days a week with Junior going to daycare and Axe joining her at the clinic. It was good for both of them. The toddler got to socialize, and she was able to return to the job she loved.

The walk was made even more enjoyable by the pleasure that Axe got from it. The dog's nose worked overtime as they passed houses and then shops. Ali had worried that he would miss working with Mike and the team. However, he seemed more than content in his role as Junior's guardian. He trotted alongside the stroller, sticking his head in every now and then to check on his charge.

Ali had finished her coffee when they arrived at the

daycare center. She unstrapped Junior, and he took off at lightning speed, heading straight for the jungle gym. She smiled. He was so much like his father, always charging off on another adventure.

She checked in with the staff before starting home with Axe and the stroller. The dog wore a worried expression, glancing back over his shoulder every few feet.

"It's OK, Axe. He's going to be fine."

As they moved across the parking lot Axe's attention returned to his surroundings, and Ali's thoughts turned to her day at the clinic. Today, she was expecting a broad range of patients: two Labradors, a Cocker Spaniel and a Chihuahua.

Axe interrupted her thoughts when he stopped dead and let out a low growl. Ali turned in the direction he was looking and wound his lead in a little tighter. "What is it, boy?"

There were a handful of cars in the parking lot and no pedestrians. Axe seemed to be fixated on a white sedan that had pulled in only moments earlier. The vehicle drove slowly, seemingly searching for a park. It passed two empty spots then exited onto the main road. Once it was gone Axe relaxed and sat on his haunches.

Ali knelt beside him and stroked his neck. "You didn't like that car, did you, buddy?"

He licked her cheek, and Ali chuckled. "OK, let's get to work." The rest of the walk home was uneventful, and soon they were on their way to her practice. She considered ringing Mike and telling him about the incident in the parking lot. But, she quickly pushed the idea from her mind. Axe had been through a lot in his life; he was allowed to have a little outburst every now and then.

Meanwhile, a little over twelve miles away at Halsey Field, Coronado Naval Base, Mike and his teammates, Rick and Ernie, were dressed in combat fatigues as they checked their equipment. Behind them, sailors were preparing an eleven-meter Rigid Hull Inflatable Boat (RHIB) for parachute insertion.

The SEALs had laid their gear out on the floor of a hangar so they could double-check their mission essential kit. Parachutes, wetsuits, combat harnesses, fins, radios, weapons, NVGs, batteries and helmets were inspected and accounted for.

Rick, a muscle-bound African American, checked his watch as he sipped from a can of energy drink. "Where's TJ? Not like pops to be late."

Chisel-jawed with a shaved head, Rick was the team's Corpsman. The former ladies' man had found love when Mike's bachelor party had gone badly wrong in the wilds of an Oregon forest.

"His wife was dropping him off," added Ernesto, or Ernie as his friends called him. The compact Latino was the team's comms guy and a family man with two boys.

"Deborah is going to drop him off at work?" asked Mike, as he adjusted the straps on his gear bag.

"I know, essé. Been on team with the guy for six years and I think I've met his wife twice."

"Doing better than me, I've never met her," added Rick as he finished the energy drink and crushed it.

"I met her once," said Mike.

"In my mind I picture her being statuesque," said Rick.

Mike shook his head. "Statuesque? Since when do you use words like statuesque to describe a woman?"

Rick tossed the can in the trash. "What? I just picture the Chief with someone empowered and yet elegant."

Mike and Ernie started at him in disbelief.

"There's something wrong with you." Mike finished with his gear. "I'm going to check the team rooms. The Chief might have gotten caught up."

Ernie gestured to the RHIB, where the riggers were making the final adjustments to the boat. "As soon as these guys are done we're supposed to be airborne."

Mike nodded and strode out of the hangar toward the team rooms. As he rounded the corner he spotted TJ unloading bags from a Mercedes sedan in the parking lot. A tall woman in an elegant suit stood at the driver's door of the car, Deborah.

Mike paused as TJ slung his bag over his shoulder and slammed the trunk. He watched as the veteran SEAL walked to his wife and stopped two feet from her. Mike couldn't hear what was being said, but from Deborah's body language it wasn't a fond farewell. She had her arms folded in front of her chest and was tapping her foot impatiently.

Feeling like he was intruding, Mike turned and returned to the hangar.

"You find him?" asked Ernie.

"Yeah, he's on his way."

"How's Junior and Ali doing?" asked Rick as he joined them.

"Good, bud. Junior's in daycare now and Ali's back at work."

"How's Axe handling that?"

"He's been heading to the surgery with Ali."

"I bet he's missing team life," added Ernie.

TJ appeared at the hangar entrance with his gear bag slung over his shoulder. With a square jaw and craggy features the Chief looked every bit the veteran operator that he was. A team guy through and through he'd been kicking doors and driving boats for over twenty years.

"How's it hanging, Chief?" Rick asked as TJ dumped his gear on the floor.

The squad leader fixed him with an icy stare. "What the hell is that supposed to mean?"

Rick swallowed. "Nothing, just wanted to know how you're doing."

"I'm fine. Got all your gear?"

"Team's fully accounted for," replied Ernie. "Your stuff is over next to mine."

"And the boat?"

"Riggers are finishing up now," added Mike.

"Good, soon as they're done load up and we'll get going." TJ strode across to his own equipment, leaving the boys to check on the boat.

"What the hell's wrong with him?" asked Rick in a low voice.

"He probably missed his coffee, you know how he gets," answered Ernie as he checked the shackles that attached the bundle of parachutes to the rubber boat.

"Yeah, grumpy as hell."

"Hey, how's Jenny going at her new job?" Mike said steering the conversation away from TJ.

Rick grinned. "She loves it. Very different to up north, but still plenty of critters to look after." His girlfriend was a park ranger.

"And the apartment, how you going with a woman in the house?"

He shrugged. "All good."

"All good?"

157

"OK, OK, I like it. She's great company and damn can she cook."

Mike turned to Ernie and smirked, the Latino winked and started whistling a tune. It took him a moment to realize it was Beyonce's *Single Ladies*.

"Quit grab-assing and get that damn boat loaded!" bellowed TJ from the other side of the hangar.

"Jeez, he is shitty," added Rick as he waved a cargo loader forward.

"Yeah," murmured Mike as he watched his squad leader stuff gear into a dive bag.

"Well, let's hope he chills out on the flight. Otherwise, this is going to be a long job."

Signed SEAL'd and Delivered:
Chapter Two

Vincent Barbosa sat cuffed with his hands shackled to a stainless steel table in a prison visitor's cell. The former cartel kingpin, known as *The Butcher*, wore a bright orange jumpsuit. A thick mustache adorned his face along with a smug look as he stared up at the security camera in the corner of the room.

"What's the holdup?" He shook his chains and spat into the corner.

A moment later there was a rattle from the room's steel door and it swung open, revealing a middle-aged man dressed in an ill-fitting suit, clutching a brown suitcase. Past his shoulder Barbosa caught a glimpse of a burly prison guard.

"You've got five minutes," barked the guard.

Barbosa's lawyer knew the drill. He scurried into the room and sat in the chair opposite, opening the briefcase to remove paperwork and a pen. "Sir, I've got some documents for you to sign."

"The usual?"

"Yes." He took an envelope from the case. "I also have a letter from your wife and children. I spoke to them this morning. They are well and send their love." The lawyer shot a look at the camera in the corner of the room as he slid the pen and documents across.

He took the pen and scribbled his signature in the required places.

The lawyer watched, glancing up at the camera every few seconds.

Barbosa leaned forward so he could tuck the letter from his family into the top pocket of his jumpsuit. "How is the plan progressing?"

The lawyer held up his hand as he rechecked the camera. As he did, it swiveled until the lens was facing the wall. He checked his watch. "OK, now we can talk. We've got two minutes before they start recording again."

"And?"

"Of course, the plan. Yes, it's progressing well. According to my sources, you will be transferred to another maximum security prison in Arizona."

"Do you have the date and time?"

The lawyer nodded. "Arrangements are being made."

Barbosa smiled. "Good, and what about my friends in San Diego, how are they?"

The lawyer swallowed. "My associate tells me they are in good health."

"Even the dog?"

"Yes, the dog is still with them."

His lip curled into a half snarl. "So nice to hear that nothing has happened to them."

The lawyer adjusted his tie. "Are we to proceed?"

"As planned."

"Very good." He checked the time. "There are other

matters we must discuss. One of your men is suspected of being an agent for the Sinaloa cartel."

"Who?"

"Eduardo Salcido."

Barbosa stared intently at the lawyer, who glanced up at the camera. "I never liked that worm. Have Duvan take care of him."

"Yes, sir." He checked his watch. "That's all we've got time for today."

The camera swiveled to face them.

The lawyer gathered up the papers. Then he rose and tucked his suitcase under his arm. "I'll see you soon."

Barbosa snorted. "I'll try to be here."

There was a familiar rattle, and the door opened. "You're done," ordered the guard.

Barbosa sat, quietly reflecting on the conversation as he waited for the guards to arrive and return him to his cell. Finally, after three long years, he was going to see vengeance for the wrongs against him. Finally, his brother Juan would get the justice he deserved.

A bell chimed as Ali pushed open the door to her favorite café, The Spanner Shop, a former garage that had been converted into a funky eatery. She spotted her sister, Leonie, at the rearmost table. The curvy brunette was sitting with a taller woman who had her back to the door, Jenny.

Athletic with almost jet-black hair, the park ranger had been dating Mike's teammate, Rick, ever since she and Ali had saved his SEAL team from red neck drug growers. She'd subsequently moved to San Diego and had become one of her closest friends. The three of them, Ali, her sister and Jenny met weekly for lunch or coffee at the café.

"Hey you," exclaimed Leonie as Ali took a seat.

"Hi guys."

"We've ordered you a coffee," added Jenny.

"Thanks, after this morning I need it."

"What's up?" asked Jenny.

"That gorgeous boy giving you trouble?" asked Leonie.

Ali shook her head. "Not at all. He's an angel, just like his dad. No, I had a rehabilitation session with a young Labrador. Eighty pounds of fur, tongue and slobber."

"Sounds like fun," said Jenny. "Where's Axe?"

"Christine took him for a walk," she replied, referring to her assistant at the practice.

A waiter arrived with a tray of coffees and placed them on the table.

"So, what's news with you?" Ali asked Jenny.

Jenny smirked as she reached out and grasped her coffee with her left hand. As she did Ali spotted a glint of light reflecting from a stone on her finger.

"No way," she squealed.

It took Leonie a split second to realize what was going on and add her own delighted screams to the cacophony. She leaped out of her chair and barged around the table. Stepping past her sister, she wrapped her arms around Jenny's athletic frame and almost crushed her. "Oh my god, that is so exciting. I'm so happy for you."

Ali managed to squeeze in and join the hug. "Congratulations, gorgeous."

When the excitement had subsided, Ali asked, "So, how did he do it? Give us all the details."

"Yes," added Leonie as she returned to her chair. "Every sordid morsel."

Jenny shot them a sheepish look as she sipped her coffee.

"What?" asked Ali.

"Oh god, don't tell me he tied it to his dick with a ribbon," exclaimed Leonie.

Jenny nearly spat out her coffee. "No, he certainly did not."

"Well come on then, spill the beans. How did San Diego's most eligible bachelor drop the question?"

"Well... he kind of didn't."

Ali gave her a sister a questioning look before turning to Jenny. "What do you mean?"

Jenny wore a cheeky smile. "I may or may not have asked him."

"Get out of town," bellowed Leonie.

"No way," added Ali. "And he said yes?"

Jenny nodded. "He even cried."

"That's adorable."

"But you can't repeat that, he'd be mortified if the boys knew. I mean they're going to give him hell when they find out we're engaged."

"They don't know?" asked Ali.

She shook her head.

"Hold the farm," said Leonie. "If you proposed, where did the ring come from?"

"He already had it."

Leonie tipped her head back and laughed. "So you got the drop on Mr. Muscles. That's the best thing ever. Now, give us the deets. You take a knee and slip a ring on his finger?"

"No, I took him out to dinner and gave him a watch."

"How did you ask?" said Ali.

She shrugged. "I just asked him if he wanted to get married."

"And?"

"And then he took a knee and said yes."

"And cried!" added Leonie.

"There was a tear or two."

"That's so damn romantic... and also kind of empowering. So, when's the date?"

"July 22, we want to get married up at the cabin."

"Back where it all began," said Ali. "It seems like yesterday we were up there saving the boy's asses."

"Seems like yesterday they were putting you through that crazy selection course," added Leonie. "Which reminds me. Did Rick pass anymore of your challenges?"

Jenny shook her head. "No, he failed the Home Depot challenge with flying colors. We both got kicked out after he wore a lamp shade as a hat."

Leonie and Ali laughed.

"That's when I realized he was the one."

Mike slipped his combat rig over his head and adjusted the side straps. Then he climbed into his parachute harness and tightened it. As he did, he glanced sideways to where Rick and the others were doing the same.

The team and their gear were squeezed in alongside the RHIB that had been loaded into a C-17 transporter. A little under an hour from their target, TJ had given them the order to suit up.

Rick was struggling to get his broad shoulders into his harness. Mike shuffled over to help him. As he yanked the straps over the Corpsman's shoulders and passed him the ends, he noticed a shiny watch on Rick's wrist.

"New bling?" he yelled over the hum that filled the cargo hold.

Rick flashed a shit-eating grin. "Jenny bought it for me."

"That's a pretty expensive gift. You guys getting serious, hey?"

"Show me that thing," demanded Ernie from where he'd appeared. The Latino hadn't started rigging up yet, having checked the boat with the loadmaster. He grabbed Rick's wrist and pulled the watch up in front of his face. "Omega Seamaster; brother that's an expensive gift. That woman's put her mark on you."

Rick snatched his arm back.

"Quit screwing around, we've got forty minutes till we're on target," TJ yelled from down the line.

"What's up his ass?" mouthed Rick.

Mike shrugged and turned his attention back to his equipment.

Thirty minutes later the team stood ready for action. TJ moved along the line, checking each of them. Then, as second-in-command, it was Mike's responsibility to inspect the Chief's gear.

He stood in front of TJ as he ran through the checklist of safety and mission essential equipment. As he inspected the clips that attached the parachute to his squad leader's shoulders, he noticed a distant look in his eyes. "Chief, you OK?"

"Yeah, I'm good. We done here?"

He gave a thumbs-up and moved back in behind him. Looking forward he focused on the loadmaster.

The ramp of the C-17 lowered with a whine that was

barely audible over the rush of air that whipped inside. Mike could now see the ocean, reaching out to the horizon behind the aircraft. He checked his watch. It was 1733 hours. They were still on schedule to get the boat in the water before dark.

The helmeted loadmaster pointed at the team and held up his palm, then gestured to the boat and raised a thumb.

A red light flashed green and the loadmaster tossed a drogue chute over the ramp. It hauled a second parachute that yanked the RHIB free of the jet. Mike watched as the massive parachute blossomed above it and the aircraft banked.

It took less than four minutes for them to loop back around. In that time the loadmaster confirmed that the boat was afloat. Then, as they leveled out, the call of thirty seconds was made.

Mike shuffled forward with his equipment braced against his legs. His pulse pounded in his ears, his breathing was shallow and muscles taut. No matter how many times he jumped, it still terrified him. Previously he'd always had the comforting bulk of Axe strapped to his front. The dog had jumped with him on more than a dozen missions and it never bothered him.

The light turned green and the loadmaster gave them the chop. Mike lurched forward after the others and stepped off the ramp into the buffeting tornado of the slipstream. There was a roar and then silence as the aircraft disappeared behind him. Free-fall was short, only a few seconds. Mike activated his chute and braced for the jerk as it deployed. Then he glanced up to check the canopy before grasping the toggles and steering for clear air.

The rest of the team was also under canopy and heading toward the boat a half-mile distant. Mike aimed toward it and enjoyed the sensation of unpowered flight.

Then, as he got closer, he cut his equipment away. It dropped to the end of its tether and hit the water.

Seconds later he splashed in and cut away his parachute. Bobbing to the surface he struggled out of his harness, detached his fins from his belt, slipped them over his boots and kicked toward the boat.

When he arrived everyone was still in the water. Rick was the first to drag himself into the RHIB. He helped the others inside and like a well-oiled machine they went to work preparing to get underway.

Minutes later they were blasting over calm waters with the sun setting behind them. TJ stood at the center console, controlling the twin marine diesels that propelled the craft at breakneck speed across the ocean. Mike stood braced against the machine gun mounting in the bow, using his sleeve to wipe the spray from his Oakleys.

After a half hour of travel TJ throttled back the engines before killing them.

"This is our rally point. We wait here till dark and then head to the beach RV." He glanced at his watch. "Sunset is fifteen minutes away. Use that time to check your kit."

Rick threw out a sea anchor then he and Ernie sat in the bow going over their gear. Mike took the opportunity to move to the stern where TJ was studying a nautical chart.

"TJ, you doing OK?"

The Chief glared at him. "Why wouldn't I be?"

He shrugged. "Just asking."

TJ turned his attention back to the map.

Mike sat on the inflatable gunnels and checked the pouches on his combat rig.

"Deb wants a divorce," TJ stated.

The news hit Mike like a punch to the chest. TJ never

talked much about his home life, but when he did it was with nothing but admiration for his wife.

The Chief's brow furrowed as he continued to look at the chart. "She says we've been apart too much. Doesn't know who I am anymore."

Mike was lost for words. He'd never seen his squad leader so vulnerable. "I'm sorry to hear that," he managed. "Have you thought of taking some time off, heading somewhere to reconnect?"

TJ nodded. "Yeah, I suggested all that. Told her we could see a counselor. She said none of it would help. It's too late."

"It's never too late. You're not going to give up are you?"

TJ looked up at him with sad eyes. "Bud, I still love her as much as the day I married her, but I don't know what I can do."

Mike leaned forward and placed a hand on his friend's shoulder. "If there's anything Ali and I can do, just ask."

"Yeah, thanks bud." The veteran SEAL glanced at his watch, then over at Ernie and Rick, who were finalizing their gear in the bow. All vulnerability disappeared from his craggy features as he thumbed the engine starter. "All right, let's get this show on the road."

Grab your copy...
vinci-books.com/seal-signed-delivered

About the Author

Jack Silkstone grew up on a steady diet of Tom Clancy, James Bond, Jason Bourne, Commando comics, and the original first-person shooters, Wolfenstein and Doom. His background includes a career in military intelligence and special operations, working alongside some of the world's most elite units. His love of action-adventure stories, his military background, and his real-world experiences combined to inspire the no-holds-barred PRIMAL series.